Priscilla looked to the sleeping baby

Helpless and beautiful, Faith made it impossible for a person not to care about her. Priscilla couldn't get attached for so many reasons. Brooks wasn't going to stay in Trout Creek, and he'd take his daughter with him when he left. Or the baby's mother would return and take her back.

Either way the baby wasn't going to stay in Priscilla's life any more than Brooks was. "She's special," she admitted, but when she turned back to him, he was staring at her.

"I was actually thinking about you."

"Me?"

His dimple flashed with a grin, and his eyes brightened despite the dark circles beneath them. "I haven't stopped thinking about you since that kiss."

Dear Reader,

I had never been very interested in sports until my daughter talked me into going to a couple of high school hockey games with her. Maybe it was because I knew some of the kids playing, but I was on the edge of my seat the whole time. Now I watch all the professional and college hockey teams play. So I just had to have a professional hockey player as a hero, and Brooks Hoover was created. He's as big a player off the ice as on, which makes him off-limits for conservative assistant principal Priscilla Andrews. Divorced Priscilla has had her heart broken once, and she doesn't intend to risk it again—on the bad boy she remembers from high school or the baby someone abandons on his doorstep.

His Baby Surprise turns Brooks's world upside down. He only intended to sit out the season back home in Trout Creek, and as soon as the team doc cleared him to play again, he was going back to the game he loved. Now his concussion is the least of his problems. He's trying to find the mother of the baby left on his doorstep and he's trying not to fall for Priscilla. He knows he'll only let her down, because he's not husband and father material even though he's become an instant daddy.

I hope you enjoy Brooks's struggle to accept his new role and responsibilities!

Happy reading!

Lisa Childs

His Baby Surprise
LISA CHILDS

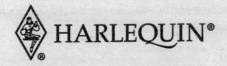

HARLEQUIN®

TORONTO • NEW YORK • LONDON
AMSTERDAM • PARIS • SYDNEY • HAMBURG
STOCKHOLM • ATHENS • TOKYO • MILAN • MADRID
PRAGUE • WARSAW • BUDAPEST • AUCKLAND

Recycling programs
for this product may
not exist in your area.

ISBN-13: 978-0-373-75305-5

HIS BABY SURPRISE

Copyright © 2010 by Lisa Childs-Theeuwes.

This edition published by arrangement with Harlequin Books S.A.

For questions and comments about the quality of this book
please contact us at Customer_eCare@Harlequin.ca

® and TM are trademarks of the publisher. Trademarks indicated with
® are registered in the United States Patent and Trademark Office, the
Canadian Trade Marks Office and in other countries.

www.eHarlequin.com

Printed in U.S.A.

ABOUT THE AUTHOR

Bestselling, award-winning author Lisa Childs writes paranormal and contemporary romance for Harlequin and Silhouette Books. She lives on thirty acres in west Michigan with her husband, two daughters, a talkative Siamese and a long-haired Chihuahua who thinks she's a Rottweiler. Lisa loves hearing from readers, who can contact her through her Web site, www.lisachilds.com, or snail mail address, P.O. Box 139, Marne, MI 49435.

Books by Lisa Childs

HARLEQUIN AMERICAN ROMANCE

1198—UNEXPECTED BRIDE*
1210—THE BEST MAN'S BRIDE*
1222—FOREVER HIS BRIDE*
1230—FINALLY A BRIDE*
1245—ONCE A LAWMAN†
1258—ONCE A HERO†
1274—ONCE A COP†

HARLEQUIN NEXT

TAKING BACK MARY ELLEN BLACK
LEARNING TO HULA
CHRISTMAS PRESENCE
  "Secret Santa"

HARLEQUIN INTRIGUE

664—RETURN OF THE LAWMAN
720—SARAH'S SECRETS
758—BRIDAL RECONNAISSANCE
834—THE SUBSTITUTE SISTER

*The Wedding Party
†Citizen's Police Academy

A special thank-you to Al Dionise and Wayne Skislak
for sharing their hockey expertise with me.
(The Knights are lucky to have you, Wayne!)
Any goofs I made about the game were totally my fault.

Chapter One

What the hell am I doing? Thirty years old and sitting in the principal's office again...

Assistant principal, Brooks Hoover corrected himself, reading the shiny brass plate on the closed door. Ms. P. Andrews. The *P* stood for Priscilla. Prissy Priscilla. Remembering the gawky girl with the horn-rimmed glasses and frizzy hair, he grinned.

Then the door opened and she stepped out of her office. Sometime during the past twelve years, she must have replaced the glasses with contacts and figured out how to tame the frizz. The strawberry-blond hair was sleek now and skimmed the line of her delicate jaw. She hadn't looked like this back in high school. The thick lenses had hidden those green eyes and high cheekbones. And now her lips were so full.

Not to mention her legs. Too bad her skirt wasn't shorter.

He shook his head. Maybe that last concussion was as serious as the doctor and trainers claimed. He had to have scrambled his brains to be ogling Priscilla Andrews, no matter how great she looked. Even as a teenager, she'd been too uptight for him. Judging from her mousy-gray suit and thin-lipped expression, she didn't appear to have changed much.

Placing his hand on the metal arm of the plastic chair, Brooks unfolded his aching bones and stood up. "Great to see you again, Pris."

Her lips pressed so tightly together that tiny lines radiated from her mouth.

"Ms. Andrews," he amended, but he couldn't keep the amusement from his voice. She had definitely not changed.

"Mr. Hoover," she replied as she extended her hand to him.

He bit the inside of his cheek to hold back a laugh at her insistence on formalities. But when he closed his hand around hers, his amusement fled. Her skin was soft, surprisingly so for someone raised in northern Michigan, where the cold weather chapped skin raw. But then, like him, she'd left Trout Creek after high school. He didn't know how long she'd been back, but her soft touch had him interested in learning more about her.

She jerked free of his grip, her eyes wide with confusion. Just how long had he been hanging on to her?

"Please step inside my office," she directed him as she walked through the doorway. Once he was inside, she closed the door behind him.

He chuckled. "This is the first time I actually asked to come to the principal's office."

"Assistant principal," she corrected. "Mr. Drover is still the principal."

"He was old when we were here," Brooks remarked. "I'm surprised he's still alive."

"Some people say the same thing about you."

"My dad's one of those people," Brooks said, remembering his father's many lectures—the most recent one coming after Brooks's last injury on the ice.

"He's not the only one," she pointed out. "Even the media keeps record of all the abuse your body has taken. The sportswriter for the county paper doesn't think you can physically handle much more."

"You can't believe everything you read," Brooks said, hoping that she didn't, even if most of what had been written about him was true.

"I'm aware of that." She picked up a note from her desk and passed it across to him.

"'Excuse my son from class today, I'm sick,'" he read aloud, grimacing at his father's forged signature. "Ryan?"

At sixteen, Ryan was the older of his two younger brothers. He doubted it would have been Brad. The fourteen-year-old was too smart to have slipped up like that.

She nodded. "If I went through Mr. Drover's files, I might find some old notes of yours. You skipped a lot of school."

"That was a long time ago," he pointed out.

"No more snowmobiling on thin ice or snowboarding down unmarked trails or—" her eyes narrowed as she tried to recall escapades he would rather forget "—drag racing down gravel roads with hairpin turns?"

"I've changed since then." That last concussion had knocked some sense into him.

Her lips curved into a slight smile. "If I believed everything I read in the papers I would doubt that."

"So you're surprised I'm still alive," he said.

"Yes," she admitted. "I went to school with you. I remember all those crazy things you did to prove how cool you were."

He flinched. What a fool he'd been. But he sure didn't remember as much about her as she did about him. "So what's with all the Ms. and Mr. crap, Pris?"

Her lips tightened into that thin line again. "You're here for an interview."

"With you?" he asked, genuinely surprised, even though the school secretary had directed him back to this office. "I thought it would be with the athletic director."

She nodded. "It is."

"You're the athletic director?" One of the few things he could remember about her from high school was that she'd been more geek than jock.

"I'm also the guidance counselor. It's a small school." She hadn't needed to remind him of that. "The budget is limited, so I have many duties here. One of which is interviewing you. Shall we get started, then?" She gestured him toward a chair in front of her desk.

"Yeah." The bright green plastic creaked as he settled onto it, and his gut constricted with regret and guilt. "I hate how this job opened up."

She nodded. "Coach Cook having a stroke was horrible."

That was an understatement. Brooks had felt like someone had hooked his skates and slammed him into the ice when he'd heard about it. He'd always figured the giant with the booming voice was invincible, like his dad.

"Do you know how he's doing?" he asked.

"I'm surprised you don't," she said. "You two were so close. In fact, he brags about you like you're his son."

That was probably more than Brooks's real father did. "I just got back in town," he explained. "I haven't had a chance to see him yet." And since he'd been pushed by his dad to go after the guy's job, he wasn't sure his old coach would want to see him.

"He's doing better," she assured him. "He's home from the rehab center. Maybe when we're done here, you can go visit him."

"Maybe…" It would be better if Coach heard the news from him. "Shouldn't we get back to the interview?"

"You're right. We need to keep this professional."

He chuckled. "This is Trout Creek, Pris. Nobody stands on ceremony in Trout Creek."

That had been part of his reason for coming back to the small town in Michigan's Upper Peninsula. Not that he was moving home to stay. After only a few days, he was restless and sick of sitting around the old house while his dad worked and his brothers—mostly— attended school. He would have headed back to his loft apartment in the city downstate if his dad hadn't reminded Brooks of the position at his old high school.

To keep from being bored out of his mind, he could coach while he waited out his suspension. Then, once the doc cleared him to play, he'd be back in the game.

"I do," she said.

Brooks shrugged. She probably wanted to establish the fact that she was going to be the boss in this relationship.

"Okay, I guess this is all just a formality, anyway, right? You're going to give me the job." His dad and the guys at the coffee shop had assured him that as someone who'd played professionally, he was the best candidate. They'd even suggested he'd be better than Coach Cook, who'd struggled with the team the past couple of years.

"Actually, no," she replied.

He tensed. She might as well have stolen the puck right off his stick.

"What! You're turning me down?"

PRISCILLA BARELY restrained the urge to laugh at him; he'd been laughing at her since she'd opened her office door. Cocky, arrogant and handsome as hell with his curly brown hair and dark eyes, Brooks Hoover wasn't used to hearing no. He probably hadn't heard that word since he'd lived in Trout Creek. And the only person who had ever told him no back then was his dad. No one else could resist his charm.

Would she have been able to if he had ever turned it on her? Probably not, she admitted to herself, heat rushing to her face. She would have been as flattered as every other girl he'd flirted with. But he had never flirted with her. He'd barely noticed her at all, just as an awkward nerd he'd liked to tease.

Prissy Pris…

It hadn't been the most imaginative nickname. But then, she wouldn't have expected anything clever from a brain-dead, daredevil jock.

"Why won't you hire me?" he demanded, his jaw taut.

"You don't want this job," she said.

He snorted. "You should have told me that earlier. I wouldn't have bothered filling out an application and getting those letters of recommendation."

"Why did you bother?" she asked. "Seeing as how this interview was just a *formality* and all?" He was so arrogant he must have figured she'd beg him to take the job—just because he'd gained a little notoriety and success since leaving Trout Creek.

"I know that in order to let me work with kids, you need references," he replied, "and a background check."

"But why would you *want* to work with kids?" She couldn't have been more shocked when the school secretary placed his application on her desk. Brooks Hoover applying for a position at Trout Creek High? It made no sense. She hadn't forgotten his vow that as soon as he graduated he was leaving and never coming back to their boring, backwoods hometown.

"I want to work with hockey players," he said, as if the athletes on the school team weren't kids. "I want to coach them."

"Why do you want to coach? Don't you want to play anymore?" She had read the articles about him, not because she was really interested but because he was a hometown boy who'd made good. Or famously bad sometimes, like when he was suspended for fighting on the ice and arrested for fighting off it. "You got demoted from the national league, but you're still playing for that city team, right?"

"Demoted? We don't call it a demotion." His deep voice was sharp with wounded pride. "I got traded." He shrugged, his broad shoulders rippling beneath his shirt. "Players move around all the time."

"From team to team. But you're not in the national league anymore."

"Not this season," he admitted. "But I can get called back up."

"Not if you're here coaching instead of playing," she pointed out.

"I can't play," he confessed with a heavy sigh. "I'm out the rest of the season."

"Suspended?"

His jaw shifted, a muscle twitching beneath the stubble. He hadn't even bothered to shave, and he wore jeans and an old Trout Creek High hockey jersey. He hadn't taken this interview seriously.

She wasn't surprised, though. She doubted he took anyone or anything seriously. Except hockey.

"No, I wasn't suspended. I just have to sit out this season." That muscle twitched along his jaw again. Whatever the reason for not playing, he wasn't happy about it.

"I still don't understand why you're here," she said, gesturing at him across her desk. "Why do you want this job?"

"I'm available this season, and the school needs a coach—at least until Coach Cook recovers."

"It's not that simple." She suspected there was so

much he hadn't included on his application. For instance, the real reason he had to miss a season.

"You're overthinking things," he accused her, even though his lips curved into that cocky grin, "like you always did. It's a no-brainer, Pris, to hire me."

She shook her head. "The no-brainer would be hiring someone with no previous coaching experience to coach a high school team. A man who's never worked with kids." Remembering a particularly sexy liquor commercial he'd done six or seven years ago, when he'd been the star of the NHL, she laughed. "You really thought I'd consider a man like you to coach impressionable kids?"

"A man like me?" he asked, leaning forward in his chair. Anger flashed in his dark eyes.

"You know your reputation, Brooks." Anyone with access to a television or a newspaper knew his reputation. "Womanizing and partying do not make you a good role model."

"I thought you didn't believe everything you read," he reminded her with another flash of that grin.

"I don't. But those kids might, and they might try to emulate you." And if he turned out to have a negative influence on the students, the school board would never give her Mr. Drover's job when the principal finally retired. "I have other applicants to interview, and plenty of time before the season begins to find the right person for the position."

"Plenty of time?" he asked, his voice sharp with disapproval. "Those kids need to be conditioning now. It's already late September. And hockey isn't just a winter sport. They should be training year-round. And none of those other applicants is going to know those kids like I do," he said. "I'm sure both my brothers will make the team."

She tapped the forged note on her desk. "How well do you know your brothers?" Brooks had already been a teenager when the younger boys were born, so Ryan and Brad had been toddlers when he'd moved away. "How often have you been home since you left, Brooks?"

"I've been back," he said, then grimaced. "Not as much as my dad would have liked. But the old man brought the boys to see me play. I know my brothers, Pris."

"Unfortunately, so do I," she said. "Too well. Teachers are constantly sending them down to me."

He chuckled. "So they cause a little trouble. What else is there to do in this town? It still doesn't have a mall or a movie theater."

"That's part of the problem," she admitted. "There's not a great deal to keep them busy, so they find ways to get into trouble—the same kind of things you did. They've heard the stories, and they want to be just like you."

"And you obviously don't think that's a good thing." His brows lowered, and the scar across the bridge of his nose formed a hard ridge.

She shook her head. "You didn't care about learning anything off the ice. These kids need to focus on their schoolwork, on their classes—not just hockey. Even you can't play sports forever."

"Hey!" he protested, his face flushed with indignation.

"You're sitting out this season," she reminded him. "That's proof these kids need to concentrate on their education because they can't count on a future in sports. Trout Creek High is all about academics now." Not everyone could be a great athlete, but they could all be successful students.

He snorted in derision. "It's still all about winning. That hasn't changed. Is Mr. Drover in today?"

"No, he's not." She leaned across her desk, struggling to control her irritation. "I'm the athletic director and I'll hire the person who's best qualified for the job."

"And that's not me?"

Hell, no. She shook her head again.

He sighed and stood slowly, with another grimace, as if weary of arguing with her. Planting his palms on her desk, he leaned across it.

Priscilla sucked in a breath, reeling from the proximity of his handsome face. The injuries over the years—the scar on his nose and above one eyebrow, and another near the cleft on his chin—only added to his sexiness. She needed to shove her chair back, to gain some distance from him. But she couldn't betray her reaction. He was already too damn cocky.

His voice husky with the anger he was notorious for unleashing on his opponents and pushy reporters, he warned her, "You're going to regret this."

Not trusting her voice to be steady enough for a reply, she just gave a slight shrug. She would have regretted hiring him and having to work with him— much more than she'd regret being one of the first women to tell Brooks Hoover no.

Chapter Two

Brooks was having a hell of a day. He'd gone straight from the principal's office to the sheriff's. With a sigh, he dropped into the chair in front of his dad's desk. This office, with its dark paneling and furniture, could not have been more different from the light walls and bright plastic furniture of the assistant principal's office.

He hadn't expected Pris Andrews to be so tough. She'd been brutal—brutally honest—and she was right. He should have paid more attention to his education. But back then he hadn't realized he wouldn't be able to play hockey forever. Even now, after what the neurologist had told him, he struggled to accept the reality that he had no future in the sport, at least not the one he'd planned on having.

"So when do you start?" Sheriff Rex Hoover asked.

"I don't."

"What do you mean?" His father barked the question at him. "Did you change your mind again?"

"Again? You're the one who changed my mind," he

reminded him. "I just stopped in Trout Creek for a visit. You're the one trying to convince me to stick around."

"You got somewhere else to be?" the old man asked skeptically.

"Nope." Thanks to the concussion he'd gotten in a fight during practice, Brooks had been suspended—for medical reasons—for the entire season. One more knock to the head, and the specialists had warned of permanent brain damage.

The worn leather desk chair creaked as his dad leaned back. "I don't understand you."

Brooks chuckled with more resignation than amusement. "That's nothing new."

"What the hell were you thinking? Why'd you blow off that interview?" His dad's face and bald head flushed red with temper.

"I didn't."

"What?" His father looked confused. "You went to the interview, but you didn't get the coaching position?"

"That's right." His body tensed as he remembered Priscilla's rejection, and he jumped up from the chair, wincing as his still-healing ribs protested the sudden movement.

"But that makes no sense." His dad shook his head. "You spent six years in the NHL."

Six years of playing too hard, too aggressively, had taken its toll on his body. He wasn't able to skate as fast as he once had, and had lost his NHL contract because of that. Now he was lucky to play for the River City league.

"I haven't played in the NHL for a few years," Brooks reminded his father.

"With all your hockey experience, she still won't find a better coach than you for the Trout Creek team."

Brooks forced a cocky grin. "She'll find a better role model, though. She doesn't want me warping those impressionable young minds."

"You need to convince her you're the best man for the job—that you've changed."

First Brooks had to convince himself of that. He shrugged. "Her mind seemed pretty made up."

His father chuckled. "Turn on your charm then, boy."

"My charm is what got me into the mess I'm in right now," Brooks reminded him. He'd had his head slammed into the ice for dating a teammate's girl. In his own defense, he'd believed her when she'd said Graham had dumped her. Turned out the goalie hadn't. But Brooks shouldn't have gone out with her anyway. "And my charm sure as hell won't work on a woman like Priscilla Andrews."

The old man sighed. "The boys call her Miss Priss."

Yeah, his brothers were idiots just as he'd been. "And that's probably another reason she won't hire me," Brooks pointed out. "She doesn't have much love for any Hoover."

"You're probably right," the sheriff admitted. "Thanks to your brothers, I've had to deal with Miss Andrews quite a bit over the past couple of years. She's a stubborn one."

Brooks studied his father. Since he'd been gone, the old man had actually gotten old. He was still a badass, with his shaved head and muscular build, but more lines rimmed his eyes and mouth. Sheriff Hoover was used to getting people—with the exception of his ex-wife and his own kids—to do what he wanted.

The thought of the old man trying to intimidate Priscilla didn't sit well with Brooks. "You're not going to do anything."

"No, you are," his father ordered. "You're going to talk to Principal Drover. Hell, you'll talk to the school board, if you have to. Half of 'em were at coffee this morning at the inn. They all expected you to get the job."

Brooks shook his head, then quickly closed his eyes as pain radiated throughout his skull. God, he couldn't make any sudden movements without repercussions. The damn doctor might have been right to recommend his medical suspension. "No, I'm not going to do that."

Pris had probably been right to deny him the job. He had no business coaching anyone until he got things under control in his own life.

"You don't care about your brothers?" his dad asked, his voice gruff with emotion. "She's already suspended Ryan twice and threatened expulsion if he screws up again."

Brooks stepped closer to the sheriff's battered desk. "So are you saying you need my help?"

"Times have changed from back when you were a kid," his father remarked, avoiding a direct answer. "There's this zero-tolerance policy now. It doesn't matter how good an athlete is, a school—namely Miss Andrews—isn't going to look the other way anymore. Kids gotta get decent grades to play sports. They can't fight. They can't skip. They gotta follow the rules."

"I can't change policy," Brooks pointed out. The only thing he knew about rules was how to break them.

"But you can encourage your brothers to behave."

Brooks risked more pain and shook his head again. "And they'd call me a hypocrite. They're smart." Remembering the forged note, he amended, "Smart-asses."

His father chuckled. "So you're going to give up that easily? And do what—take off again?"

"I did not run away," Brooks insisted, refusing to let his father guilt him. He'd felt bad enough leaving his dad to raise his younger brothers alone—as if he'd deserted them the same way their mother had. "I got a college scholarship, then drafted into the NHL. I have a job. A life. I do have somewhere I need to be." An empty apartment with friends who would be too busy training to spend any time with him.

"Do you have someone special?" his father asked.

He chuckled. "Lots of someones special," he replied, more to annoy his father than because it was the truth. Sure, he dated a lot, but casually. He'd figured out a long time ago that he wasn't the forever kind of guy.

"So you're a player off the ice, too?"

Brooks shrugged. "At least I never get bored."

Immediately, he regretted the comment. His mother had taken off because she'd grown bored with Trout Creek, with marriage and motherhood. While his dad had never made the comparison, Brooks knew he was just like his mother. He'd felt suffocated in this damn town. He shouldn't have let his dad manipulate him into applying for that position.

"We can't do this," he pointed out with quiet resignation. "You and I—we still rub each other the wrong way. We can't get along."

But when he'd awakened from the three-day coma following his head injury, he'd opened his eyes to find his father standing over his bed. And he'd seen the profound relief and love on his old man's face. No matter how much they fought, his father cared about him—cared what happened to him as no one else in Brooks's life ever had. And that love had drawn Brooks home to Trout Creek. But he was already too restless to stay.

ANGER FLUSHED PRISCILLA'S skin with such heat that she'd shrugged out of her jacket in the car. Despite the late September breeze, she wasn't cold. She was hot with fury. She lifted her hand and pounded on the door of the Hoovers' sprawling ranch house, since Brooks ignored the bell.

He was definitely home. The dust-covered black Ford Mustang parked in the gravel driveway was his. Word of how "cool" it was, with its spoiler and chrome wheels, had spread all over the school. But what he'd done since leaving her office that morning was definitely not cool with Priscilla.

Finally, the door opened, and afternoon sunlight gleamed off the smooth skin of a heavily muscled chest and arms. Her gaze involuntarily followed the drops of water that fell from his curly wet hair to his shoulders, trailing down his chest and washboard abs to disappear into the unsnapped waistband of his jeans. Now she was hot for another reason.

"Did you change your mind?" he asked.

She dragged in a quick breath, which she regretted as his fresh-from-the-shower scent filled her senses. She'd never been more certain that she was right. Brooks Hoover would not be a good influence on the impressionable teenagers—let alone her.

"You didn't give me the chance," she said, summoning her anger to squash her irrational attraction to him. It wasn't really about him, anyway; it was just that she'd been back in Trout Creek too long, where the only single men were senior citizens or minors.

Brooks sighed, stepped back and gestured for her to come inside. Hoping he'd finish getting dressed before he explained his actions to her, Priscilla joined him in the narrow foyer. She tripped over a pile of oversized sneakers, and he caught her arm. Holding tight to her elbow, his hip bumping against hers, he led her down the hall to the living room, which was as cluttered as the foyer. Every available surface was covered, and in the center a mound of newspapers, pop cans and food wrappers buried what must have been a coffee table.

"Myrtle comes in tomorrow," Brooks said, referring to Trout Creek's only cleaning woman. He picked up some discarded shirts and a couple handheld games to clear a chair for her.

Priscilla shook her head, too angry to sit when she wanted to pace. But there wasn't much available floor space. "I feel sorry for her," she remarked, wishing he would put on one of the shirts he'd picked up. Instead, he dropped them onto the table.

"You didn't come here to talk about Myrtle," he reminded her. "And I'm not sure what you mean. You were the one who didn't give me a chance, by not hiring me."

"But that didn't stop you. You went over my head and got the job for yourself." His action had also earned her a lecture from her boss, who had trusted her judgment until now.

"I didn't go over your head," he insisted. "Nobody's hired me."

Confusion cooled her temper slightly. "So no one has told you yet? Well, let me be the first to congratulate you."

He pushed a hand through his damp hair, tangling the dark curls. "I—I had no idea...."

"You really didn't," she said, as realization dawned. "I don't understand what happened, then. I didn't even have a chance to tell Principal Drover my decision before he called me."

Brooks expelled a weary sigh. "Damn him."

"Who?"

"I told my dad," he replied. "If anyone went over your head..."

Sheriff Hoover. Ever since Ryan had started high school, she'd had almost as many problems with the father as the son. Rex Hoover did not want to admit that his boys were not just "being boys" when they skipped school and got into fights. Having dealt with overprotective parents before, she understood why Rex would defend his teenage sons. But Brooks? He was the same age she was—thirty or close to it.

Her gaze skimmed over him again, all six foot plus

of sinewy muscle. He was definitely not a boy. She laughed. "You told your daddy on me?"

"It wasn't like that." He sounded irritated. "I just let him know how the interview went. I didn't want him to do anything about it."

"You don't even want this job," she said with sudden understanding. "Your dad pushed you into applying." She shook her head. "This is going to be worse than I thought. You're going to be like those kids whose parents force them into joining the band. They lose their instruments or try to break them, anything to get out of playing."

That cocky grin flashed again. "I'm not going to break anything."

She wasn't so sure about that. With his bad-boy charm and good looks, he would definitely break a few hearts when he left Trout Creek again.

"How long are you even planning on sticking around?" she asked.

"I'll see the season through."

She turned away from him, unable to think coherently with so much of his bare skin showing. Through an open door, she glimpsed a suitcase lying open on a bed. "You were already packing to leave."

"I didn't think I had a reason to stay."

Now she understood why the sheriff had gone to such extremes to get Brooks the position; he wanted his oldest son home.

"This is a mistake," she murmured.

"I know you have concerns," he said, cupping her shoulders and turning her back to face him.

Her skin tingled beneath his rough palms, and she wished she'd left on her jacket. She stepped back, so that his hands dropped to his sides. "You really need to withdraw your application. You're not qualified for this job. You have no coaching experience."

A muscle twitched in his cheek. "I know hockey. I could barely walk when I strapped on my first set of skates."

"Coaching is more than that," she argued. "You have to know how to deal with kids."

Brooks had to figure out how to deal with Priscilla first—since he apparently worked for her now. His dad going over her head did not help the situation any. He thought of Rex's advice to charm her. Hell, he couldn't even touch her without her jerking away from him. He'd barely had a moment to register the softness of her skin.

"Brooks," she said impatiently, as if she'd called to him once or twice already.

He shook his head, hating how dazed he'd felt since waking up from that concussion-induced coma. "Yeah?"

"Do you have *any* experience with children?"

He could have reminded her that he'd helped his dad with his younger brothers, but that had been a dozen years ago. "Not really."

"Then you must understand how unqualified you are to coach a high school team. I have a master's degree in adolescent psychology and I still struggle to handle them."

Her justified doubts resurrected the argument he'd given his father when Rex had first suggested to

Brooks—no, commanded him—to apply for the position. The ever-present dull ache in his head intensified to a sharp hammering. When the peal of the doorbell rang out, echoing throughout the house, he flinched.

"Someone's at the door," he unnecessarily pointed out. At least he was saved from answering her question.

"Probably someone to congratulate you on your new job," she remarked sarcastically.

He stepped around her and crossed the foyer, dirt grinding beneath his bare feet. With three—four now—guys in the house, Myrtle needed to clean more than once a week. He jerked open the door to the afternoon sunshine and nothing else.

"Hello?" he called.

The house was a little far out in the country for someone to play the ring-the-bell-and-run game. He glanced at the pines that towered around the house, and the winding gravel driveway. Only one vehicle, a practical, dust-colored station wagon, sat behind his Mustang; it had to be Priscilla's.

"Hello?" he called again.

A soft cry drew his attention down to a blanket-covered bundle on the front step. A sense of foreboding rushed over him like the early autumn breeze, chilling his skin. He bent down and lifted the pink fleece blanket.

His breath escaped in a gasp as he stared down at the baby strapped into the car seat. Someone had left a baby on his doorstep? A bib tied around her neck proclaimed her Daddy's Girl.

But who was Daddy?

Chapter Three

Pine needles and gravel bit into the soles of his bare feet as Brooks limped back to the house. The car seat still sat on the step, the baby squirming as she awakened with quiet cries.

"You didn't see anyone?" Priscilla asked.

"No." He sighed. "I didn't hear a car, so I checked the closest snowmobile trail." Several of them wound through the woods surrounding the house. "But I didn't see anyone." Just a deer that had been as startled as he was. "The trees and brush are thick, though." Someone could have easily been hiding out there, watching him and the house and the infant.

He crouched down and studied the baby more closely. She had perfectly shaped rosebud lips, a little dimple in her left cheek and a dark fuzz of hair that already looked as if it was going to curl. Along with a flash of recognition, that sensation of foreboding rushed over him again, chilling his bare skin.

"Who...who would just leave a newborn this way?" Priscilla asked, her voice cracking with emotion. Then she turned to him, and her green eyes widened with regret and sympathy. "Oh, I'm sorry. I didn't think…."

"About my mom?" he asked. "Yeah, Brad wasn't much older than this when she took off for good." Dread tightened his stomach as he realized that this infant looked exactly the same as Brad and Ryan had as babies. He groaned. "Oh, no…"

"Your mom has to be beyond childbearing years," Priscilla assured him.

"I wasn't thinking about my mom," he replied. But he was trying to think—to fight through the fog the concussion had left of his memories—to figure out who this baby's mother could be.

"Your dad?" she asked, her voice squeaking with shock.

He laughed. "No. Not my dad."

"Then whose is she?"

He swallowed back the emotion and fear that threatened to overwhelm him. "I—I think she might be mine."

As if she was as horrified as he was at the thought he could be her father, the baby released a high-pitched cry. Her body tensed against the straps of the car seat and she lifted her fisted hands, punching at the air. The kid was definitely a Hoover. His dad claimed that every one of them had come out swinging.

Brooks glanced from the baby's face, which was growing red with frustration, to Priscilla's, which was eerily pale. Apparently she was as stunned as he was by his admission. Too stunned to react to the baby's cry for attention. But just because she was female didn't mean she had any maternal instincts.

Hell, when it came to kids, he had no instincts at all. His hands shook as he unclasped the straps that secured the baby into the carrier. He hadn't held a newborn in fourteen years, and while his brothers had looked uncannily similar to this baby, they'd never been as small and seemingly fragile.

But they had been this loud. The baby's cry increased in volume and desperation. His head still pounding, Brooks winced as much in commiseration as pain. Poor kid…

"How do you do this?" he asked, sliding his hands beneath the tiny tense body. "How do I pick her up?"

Priscilla expelled a shaky little breath and started directing him. "Cradle her head. Infants' necks aren't strong enough to hold them up."

He held his breath as he lifted the baby, careful to palm her delicate head. That soft dark hair, which was barely long enough to curl, brushed his skin. The baby blinked and stared up at him, focusing on his face. Her eyes were dark and already fringed with lashes. Did babies this young have eyelashes that long?

God, she was beautiful.

"She stopped crying," Priscilla whispered.

He'd been staring at her so intently, studying her perfect, miniature features, that he hadn't realized she'd fallen silent. But a single tear slid down the side of her dimpled cheek to pool in his palm.

"Wh-why do you think she was crying?" he asked, his heart contracting at the thought of the child being in pain. She was so tiny, unable to protect herself. She had to rely on adults being there for her. Poor kid…

"She's probably scared."

She wasn't the only one. He had that familiar old pressure in his chest, the one he'd felt back in his teens, when he'd worried that he would never get out of Trout Creek.

"Or hungry." Priscilla crouched down next to the carrier and picked up a diaper bag. "There's formula, bottles and some diapers in here. Are you sure someone just rang the bell and left her?"

"I looked all around," he reminded her. "I didn't see anyone."

"If you think this baby is really yours, you need to call the mother and talk to her—find out if she's the one who left the baby."

"Who else could have left her but her mother? Especially like this, with the car seat and the diaper bag." And the little bib that called her Daddy's Girl.

"It probably was the mother," Priscilla agreed. "All the more reason you have to see her and find out what's going on."

With an inward grimace, he admitted, "I don't know who the mother is."

"Brooks…"

He didn't need to look at her to see the disgust on Priscilla's face. It was there in her voice. He could have used the concussion as an excuse, but it wasn't to blame for his not being able to remember who the baby's mother was. He had dated a lot. Still, he struggled to understand how he could have possibly become a father. "I always use protection."

"It's not one hundred percent effective," Priscilla said.

As assistant principal, she had probably given more than her share of safe-sex lectures. As his father's son, Brooks had already heard more than enough.

"It's a little late and I'm a little old for your abstinence speech, Ms. Andrews."

She laughed. "I wouldn't waste my breath giving it to you. But why do you think the baby is yours?"

He studied that perfect little face. Even though she'd quieted down and was staring up at him, her fists still moved in little air punches, filling him with that same sense of recognition. "I just…"

"Can't know for certain—this is the sheriff's house," she pointed out. "Maybe someone was just abandoning the baby to the local authority."

Brooks wished he could believe that, but he shook his head. "Then they would have left her at his office, not his house. He's not even home. Hell, the only cars in the driveway are ours. Unless the kid is yours…?"

She gasped.

"Sorry, bad joke." He quickly apologized, wondering about the panic that flashed in her eyes. She worked with kids but had an aversion to babies? He suspected there was a lot more to Priscilla Andrews than he would ever know.

"You can't be certain that she's yours, either," she stubbornly maintained.

"No," he agreed. But his gut—the one that had guided him to every winning shot—told him the baby was his.

"You're a relatively high-profile athlete and pretty notorious for your playboy ways," she said with that disapproval again. "I'm sure you've had previous paternity suits."

He snorted. "Gee, boss, your opinion of me is so high." Unfortunately, it was pretty damn accurate. "But you're wrong about one thing. I've had no previous paternity suits. Like I said, I always use protection."

"You need a DNA test."

Gravel ground under rubber as a car headed down the driveway. "Maybe she's coming back," he said, the tightness easing in his chest. But then disappointment flashed as he stared down into those alert, innocent eyes. She was such a pretty baby.

"It's your dad," Priscilla informed him.

A door creaked open, then slammed shut again. The baby tensed in Brooks's hands and began to cry again.

"Shhh…" He tried to soothe her, cradling her closer to his body.

"What the hell—" Rex's jaw snapped open in shock. "Whose baby is that?"

As Priscilla had suggested, he needed a DNA test to prove it, but even knowing his father's disapproval would surpass hers, Brooks had to confess what his gut was telling him. "Mine."

NUMB WITH SHOCK, Priscilla stared out the window of the bus. Since the nights were already growing longer in northern Michigan, there was nothing to see but the occasional animal's eyes glinting in the dark along the country road. She was supposed to be chaperoning the football players and cheerleaders as they traveled home from an away game. That was the excuse she'd given to rush off from the Hoovers' house that afternoon. As the athletic director, she was responsible for the entire sports program and was expected to appear at every match, meet and game.

Tonight was the first time she had really appreciated that responsibility. The raised voices and raucous laughter of the victorious kids kept her from her own thoughts and from the long-ago memories she didn't want to revisit.

She shifted as someone dropped into the seat beside her. Welcoming the distraction, she turned away from the window. She'd expected one of the cheerleaders, but instead found a reminder of the man and the baby she was trying to forget. "Brad."

The youngest of the Hoovers, at least until now, had the same mop of dark curls, dimples and dark eyes as his oldest brother—and that baby someone had abandoned on their doorstep. "Hey, Miss A. So did you give my brother Coach Cook's old job?"

Despite being a freshman, Brad played on the varsity football team. His speed made him a natural quarterback, but his real love was hockey. Just as it had been with Brooks.

"No," she replied honestly.

"But—but why not?" the boy sputtered, his face flushing a deeper shade of red than it had from the exertion of scoring the winning touchdown in the close game.

"He's not qualified," she explained.

"But he was a pro player."

"But he's never been a coach."

"So?" the boy challenged, his dark eyes full of anger.

"His lack of coaching experience didn't make him the right candidate for the job," she patiently explained.

The same way she'd done to her boss when Principal Drover had questioned, then overruled, her decision. He, as well as most of the members of the school board, was friends with the sheriff; they had coffee every morning at the Trout Creek Inn.

"That's stupid." Brad didn't conceal his disgust. "And it's probably why he didn't show up for the game tonight." Disappointment dimmed the boy's eyes. He idolized his older brother, but he'd only been a toddler when Brooks left home, and the truth was, Brad barely knew him. "He probably took off already. That's why Dad didn't show up, either. He won't be happy if Brooks left."

She knew why Brooks and their father had missed the game, but it wasn't her place to tell Brad that he and Ryan might have become uncles. The boy scrambled out of the seat before she could say anything to allay his fear. For all she knew, despite the baby's arrival or maybe because of it, Brooks might have left town already.

As if she could feel their angry stares, she glanced to the back of the bus, where Brad had rejoined his brother Ryan. The sixteen-year-old had the same curly hair and dark eyes, but his build was bigger than his brothers'. So he played defense on both the football and hockey teams.

As they glared at her, Priscilla was the one who felt defensive. Even though she'd been overruled, she'd done the right thing in not hiring Brooks. He was about as qualified to be a coach as he was to be a father.

How angry would he be when he learned what she'd done after leaving his house that afternoon?

SHE'D CALLED A DAMN social worker on him. Brooks
cursed at the pain radiating from his knuckles, which
oozed blood. With another curse, he tossed the wrench
onto the floor.

A cry pierced the air and another curse followed it,
but this one came from his father's lips. "Damn it, I just
finally got her to sleep."

"Now there'll be somewhere to put her when she
falls asleep again," Brooks said, as he scooted out from
beneath the crib he'd just assembled. Pressing down
with his hands on the wooden sides, he tested the stur-
diness of the little bed, and a sense of satisfaction shot
through him. He'd proved one of Priscilla's claims to
the social worker wrong.

Granted, he hadn't been prepared for a baby showing up on his doorstep, but that could be fixed. After
having her checked out at the hospital in the city, he and
his dad had stopped at a department store for the things
Rex had promised the social worker they'd buy for her:
a bed, a changing table, more clothes, more formula
and diapers.

Boxes and bags overflowed the room where Brooks
had spent his childhood. His suitcase still lay open on
the bed, the few things he'd brought with him already
packed. His worn jeans and old jerseys looked out of
place in what had essentially become a baby nursery.

Noticing the suitcase, his dad remarked, "You should
take care of that."

If Brooks put it where he wanted, it would be in the
trunk of his car as he fled Trout Creek. "Here." He

reached instead for the baby wailing in his father's arms. "I can try to rock her back to sleep."

The ancient rocker, with its wicker seat and back, had been the first thing they'd dragged in from the living room. Rex sat in it now, wearing only an undershirt, because the baby had soaked his khaki sheriff's shirt. With more ease and grace than Brooks could manage, the old man rose from the chair and handed off the crying baby.

Brooks struggled to support her neck and hang on to her tense body. That panic pressed on his chest again. "What's wrong with her?"

"Maybe she's upset that Priscilla Andrews called the social worker on us," his dad replied sarcastically. Obviously he was pretty upset about it.

A county employee, Mrs. Everly had met them at the hospital. "I'm sure she was just concerned about the baby."

"Concern?" Rex snorted. "She couldn't even look at the little girl when she was here. Hell, she couldn't get away fast enough."

Brooks stared down at the squalling infant. Priscilla hadn't been comfortable around the baby; even he had noticed that. He shrugged. "I guess she had a phone call to make."

"Yeah, it backfired on her. She didn't know I had a foster home certificate."

"I didn't, either," Brooks admitted.

The old man shrugged. "As sheriff, I've had to put some drunken parents in jail overnight. If there's no place for their kids to go, I can bring them here."

His father was a good man, something Brooks hadn't

realized until that blow to the head had knocked some sense into him.

If the DNA test they'd taken at the hospital proved this baby really was Brooks's daughter, would he be able to love her as much as his dad loved him? Was he even capable?

"Shhh…" He had no idea what to call the baby. "You need a name, little girl."

"You really don't know it?" Rex asked.

He shook his head. "And I think she's too young to tell me."

His father didn't laugh at his lame attempt at a joke. Instead he began to fire questions at Brooks as if he was interviewing a suspect. "You really didn't see who left her at the door?"

"No. I looked around, but there was no one." He suspected someone had been out there, watching.

"You have no clue who the mother could be?"

"Priscilla thought the baby might have been left for you," he replied.

His dad laughed. "That's not possible."

"I heard you were dating." The boys had said something about their father going out with a woman.

Rex flushed. "That's not what I mean. I had that…little procedure years ago. I thought it might make your mom stick around."

"That wasn't the problem, though, was it," Brooks said. "She didn't want the ones she already had."

"Brooks—"

He shook his head. "Priscilla thought someone might have abandoned the baby here because you're the sheriff."

Rex stared down the infant's red face and flailing fists, and sighed. "She's a Hoover."

"Yeah." Brooks's gut had already told him the same thing.

"Trout Creek is small and gossipy," his father pointed out. "If anyone was pregnant, it would have been all over town."

Brooks winced. "Just like someone dropping a baby on our doorstep is going to be all over town. And in the papers pretty soon."

"Yeah."

Since the hockey season hadn't started yet, he'd figured he had some time before the press began to hound him, questioning why he wasn't playing. But hell, he'd rather have them think it was because of the baby than his being medically unable to play.

"I'm surprised she—whoever the baby's mother is—hasn't already gone to the press," his father remarked. "Or at least called you for child support or something."

"She's obviously not thinking clearly, to leave a baby on a doorstep. We need to find her."

His dad nodded. "Yeah, the doctor said she must have had the baby alone, the way the cord was so crudely tied off. I have calls in to the local hotels and motels, trying to track down a single woman who checked in pregnant."

Rex Hoover wasn't only a good man, he was a good sheriff. That was why he'd been elected term after term after term. If anyone could find the baby's mother, he could.

"So, do *you* have any idea where to start looking?"

his dad asked. "Can you give me a list of women you were dating nine months ago?"

His head pounded hard as he tried to remember names, faces, anything. The concussion had muddled some of his memory, but it wasn't the reason he couldn't recall past relationships. He just hadn't cared enough about anyone he'd dated. "No." Brooks stared down at the tiny red face. "But whoever she is, she'll come back for her baby." She had to.

"I thought the same thing about your mother," the old man admitted.

And she had never returned.

Brooks had spent a lot of his life blaming his father for his mother's leaving. Would his child blame him for her mother abandoning her? Was that why she cried now, because she missed her mother? Or because she instinctively sensed that he wasn't cut out for fatherhood?

He knew the admission wasn't going to please his dad, but he had to voice his fear aloud. "I can't do this."

Chapter Four

Brooks shifted the baby to his shoulder, her head and neck in one palm, her back and diapered butt in the other.

A strong hand patted his other shoulder. "Hey, you used to help me with your brothers."

"That was a long time ago," Brooks reminded him. "Brad's fourteen now. And neither he nor Ryan were ever this little."

His father shrugged. "So we might be kinda rusty."

"Should we have let the social worker take her?"

"You don't want her?" his father asked—with the disappointment Brooks remembered so well from his youth. Every crazy stunt he'd pulled had disappointed the old man.

Brooks tightened his hands on the baby's small body, and a burp slipped through her lips along with a trail of slimy spit-up that dripped down his neck. He grimaced, then grinned as her crying turned into a soft sigh of relief. "I don't know what to do."

His heart told him to stay; his head told him to run.

"Giving her a name would be a start," his dad suggested.

"I—I can't think of anything...."

"You can't think of a girl's name?" His dad chuckled. "You probably know more than most. Hell, that's what got you in this predicament."

Fatherhood. Could he really be a daddy? Brooks still had to put together the changing table, so he carried her to the bed and laid her down beside the suitcase. Then he reached for the diaper bag.

"You okay for now?" his dad asked. "Because speaking of predicaments, I need to find out where your brothers are. They should have been back from that game a while ago."

Brooks glanced at his watch. "They broke curfew?" Maybe Priscilla was right; they were trying to be just like him.

"They better not be doing anything stupid," Rex grumbled as he walked out of the room.

Being alone with the baby increased that pressure on his chest, and Brooks had to breathe deep. "I can do this," he assured her—and himself—as he pulled out a diaper. He'd watched his father change her earlier. "Tabs in the back."

First he had to pull open the snaps holding her pajama thingy closed. His fingers fumbled with the soft material until he freed her kicking legs. Then he ripped open the tabs of her soiled diaper and tried to stop breathing altogether at the pungent odor. He dumped out the diaper bag to get the wipes. A piece of paper fell onto the bed.

Forgetting the diaper for a moment, he grabbed the note, which was addressed to "Daddy."

It's time for you to grow up and take some responsibility for once. You need to stop being a self-absorbed, selfish jerk and raise your daughter.

Brooks flinched at the brutal assessment of his character, or lack thereof. It sounded like something Priscilla would write. Of course, under no circumstances would she have ever let him close enough to get her pregnant.

"Hey, Brooks—you're still here!" a young male voice shouted as the front door slammed against the foyer wall.

Startled by the commotion, the baby cried and kicked, and the soiled diaper slipped out from beneath her, its contents spreading onto the bed and the baby's clothes.

"God, it reeks in here," Ryan murmured, gagging as he stepped inside the room.

"What is all this stuff?" Brad asked, his fingers pinching the end of his nose.

"What's that?" Ryan asked, pointing toward the baby on the bed.

"Your niece," their father answered as he joined them in Brooks's very crowded bedroom.

"What? You knocked someone up?" Brad's eyes were wide as he stared at the baby.

"Where is she?" Ryan asked, backing toward the doorway. "I bet she's hot."

Hot as in pissed off, yeah. Brooks shoved the note in

his pocket. Seeing it would only disappoint his dad. "She's not here."

"What did she do—bring the baby and take off?" Brad asked.

Brooks nodded as he cleaned up the messy infant. "Dad's going to track her down, though."

"So she can take her kid back?" Ryan asked.

"I don't know about that," their father replied. "The baby will probably be better off with us."

"With us?" Brad's voice cracked with disbelief.

"*She's* staying here?" Ryan asked, clearly appalled at the thought of the baby living with them. "No way!"

"Of course she's staying," their father replied. "She's family. And we're all going to help your brother."

"So *you're* staying?" Brad asked him, glancing from the baby to the suitcase.

Brooks sighed. He didn't know how long he'd be able to stick it out in Trout Creek, but he nodded. "Sorry I missed the game tonight."

"We won!" Ryan announced, stabbing his fist in the air—exactly as the baby on the bed was doing.

"So you guys were out celebrating, then?" their father asked. "That's why you missed curfew?"

"The bus was late getting back to the school," Brad said.

"No," Rex corrected. "I checked with Wes's mom. The bus was back over an hour ago."

"We were just a little late," Ryan said. "It's not like we've got anything going on tomorrow, anyhow—since we still don't have a hockey coach."

"Yes, you do," their father announced.

"We do?" Brad asked.

"Your brother."

"But—but," Brad stammered, "Miss Priss said she didn't hire you."

"She changed her mind," the old man explained.

Because he'd had it changed for her. Brooks doubted she would ever forgive him for letting his father go over her head.

"Uh, we didn't know that," Brad said, his eyes filling with guilt.

Ryan shrugged. "Just because she changed her mind this time doesn't mean she's not still a bitch."

"Ryan!" Brooks reprimanded his brother, startling the baby. She began to cry again.

"Sheesh, she's not gonna do that all night, is she?" Ryan asked. "We should have stayed out later."

"You already broke curfew," their father reprimanded.

"Maybe she will," Brooks warned them. "You used to cry all night." Especially after their mom had taken off. Brad hadn't been much older than this baby when their mother had left. That time for good.

She'd disappeared after Brooks was born, too, and had stayed away for nearly half a decade. But then she'd returned to Trout Creek. She'd made him and his dad believe that she'd gotten her life together and was going to stick around. And she had—for several years—even after Ryan was born. But having Brad only two years later was too much for her. Or so she'd explained in the note she'd left.

"Don't worry," Brooks assured them. He was worried enough for all of them. "I'll take care of her."

"Yeah, you're doing a great job," Ryan scoffed. "What's all over your neck and your shirt? Baby puke?"

"And look at your bed." Brad's face twisted into a grimace of disgust.

Brooks lifted the baby from the mess, and the diaper slid down her legs and dropped on top of the pajama thingy he'd pulled off her.

"She's mooning you," Brad said, jabbing his elbow into Ryan's ribs.

"She's mooning *you*," Ryan retorted.

Rex laughed. "You didn't put the diaper on tight enough."

Brooks hadn't wanted to irritate the clipped cord of her little outie belly button.

"Do you even know how to change a diaper?" Ryan asked, as if horrified at the thought.

"Yeah," he snapped as he laid the baby back on the bed. "I used to change both of you. At least she can't spray me in the face the way you guys did."

"Gross," Brad said.

"It's gross in here," Ryan agreed, and the two of them headed for the door.

"Hey!" Brooks called his brothers back. Something was worrying him besides doubts over his ability to handle fatherhood. "You guys didn't do something to her place, did you?"

"Whose place?" Ryan asked, all fake innocence.

"To Priscilla Andrews's house," he clarified, studying their faces. "Did you?"

The baby let out a bloodcurdling cry. While he turned

his focus back on her, his brothers took advantage of the distraction and ran away.

He suspected there was something else for which Priscilla would hold him responsible.

PRISCILLA LIFTED HER GAZE to the canopy of trees surrounding her cabin. Toilet paper hung from several branches like streamers.

"I thought Halloween was a couple weeks away yet," her sister mused as she leaned over the porch railing next to Priscilla.

"Every day is Halloween around me," she said. This was the third time her place had been TP'd since the school year had begun. She'd lost count of the number of times last year and the year before that. Even though she'd been working at the school for five years, nothing had happened to her place until Ryan Hoover had become a freshman. "Are you sure you want to rent to me?"

"Rent? You mean you're paying me?" Maureen asked, her green eyes wide with feigned surprise.

"I've been trying to pay you," Priscilla reminded her stubborn older sister. When she'd moved back to Trout Creek, Maureen had offered her one of the guest cabins in the woods behind the fishing and hunting lodge her husband owned and managed.

Priscilla had eagerly accepted the gracious offer for a couple of reasons. One, the only other place to stay was the Trout Creek Inn, where the locals gathered for coffee and gossip every morning. She hadn't wanted to be gossiped about, or to listen to gossip about other people. The second reason she'd accepted the offer was because she'd wanted to be by herself. Secluded in the woods, away from the lodge, her little cabin was perfect for her. But its private location also made it easy for the local troublemakers to vandalize without fear of getting caught.

Maureen shrugged. "You help me out with the kids. That's more than Stan does." Stan Wieczorek was Priscilla's brother-in-law, but he wasn't much of a father to his and Maureen's four kids. He would rather fish and hunt than help with homework or bath time. And Priscilla doubted he had ever changed a diaper.

Had Brooks? Or had Rex done diaper duty last night? The social worker, Mrs. Everly, had left Priscilla a message that she'd allowed them to take the baby home, but she would be following up on the DNA test as well as their ability to care for a newborn.

The Hoovers probably thought Priscilla had called out of spite. But she'd been concerned about that tiny, helpless child. The baby needed someone responsible who could protect her from harm.

"Priscilla?" Her sister nudged her with her shoulder.

She steadied the mug of coffee Maureen had nearly made her spill and forced a smile. "I don't have to help you very much. The kids were already out of diapers by the time I came home to Trout Creek. And they're growing up so fast."

"Too fast," Maureen agreed with a sigh. She patted her hair, self-conscious of the few strands of gray that wound through the light brown.

Like Brooks and Ryan, nearly a dozen years separated Maureen and Priscilla, but they had a couple of brothers in the middle. The boys, however, had never come home to Trout Creek after leaving for college. Eventually their brother Charles had convinced their parents to move south with him and his family.

"Can you believe this is Adam's senior year?" Maureen asked, referring to her oldest son. "It seems like yesterday that I was crying over putting him on the bus and sending him off alone for his first day of kindergarten."

Priscilla felt a pang as she remembered someone who should have been starting kindergarten this year. She hadn't been able to stop thinking about her since yesterday afternoon. Needing the caffeine after her sleepless night, she drank deeply from her mug.

"Brooks Hoover called Adam this morning," Maureen said. "The kid acted all casual while he was on the phone. But he was over-the-moon excited that he'd talked to a famous hockey player."

"Brooks called Adam?"

"Yeah, he wants him down at the Icehouse to try out for the hockey team."

"What?" As athletic director, she was supposed to announce tryouts—not just to kids Brooks had chosen but the entire school. He might not have gone over her head with the hiring, but he had now.

"Yeah, he was calling everyone who was on the team last year," her sister replied. "I thought you weren't going to hire Brooks, that you didn't think he was serious about the job."

"He's not." Priscilla was certain of that, especially now. What the hell was he trying to prove? And who was he trying to prove it to—his dad or her?

"And after Brooks hung up, Stan called. He was

having coffee down at the Trout Creek Inn and heard some interesting rumors." Maureen's eyes were bright with excitement. "'Course, folks are always talking about Brooks Hoover—"

"It's true," Priscilla interrupted. "I was there when he found the baby on his doorstep."

"You were there?" Maureen asked, her voice warm with concern. "Are you all right?"

Priscilla nodded. "Sure."

"But that must be the first time you've been around a newborn since…"

Since her own baby had died. Ignoring the pain squeezing her heart, she shrugged off her sister's concern. "I'm around kids all the time."

"Teenagers. Not babies. I think that's why you moved back to Trout Creek."

"There are babies here," she pointed out. But in the five years she'd been home, she had mostly been able to avoid contact with them. She might see them around town, but she didn't have to touch them, the way Brooks had expected her to touch his…

Daughter?

Was the child really his?

When the infant had begun to cry, he'd looked at her, waiting for her to do the maternal thing and comfort the little girl. He had no idea just how unmaternal she was. She hadn't even been able to take care of her own baby.

Chapter Five

Brooks closed his eyes, unable to watch any more of the action on the ice. And calling it action was generous. The kids were barely moving. Where was the speed Trout Creek High hockey was famous for? Where were the shots? Where the hell were the blocks?

Defense.

C'mon.

He gritted his teeth to hold back the curse burning his throat. His brothers had given him the phone numbers for the kids who'd played hockey last year. But not enough had showed up even to constitute a team. And the ones who had come...

"So this is how you're going to pick your team?" a feminine voice, sharp with skepticism, asked. "You're not paying any attention to the players."

He tensed, and the baby, nestled inside his coat, wriggled. He shifted his grip, cupping her tiny head in his palm. "Shh..."

Her cheeks pink from the cold, Priscilla stepped closer to the bleachers where he stood. In jeans and a bright green coat, she looked more like one of the high school students than the assistant principal. She leaned toward him, her silky hair skimming his chin, and peeked inside his jacket. Her breath escaped in a gasp that turned to mist in the cool air between them. "You brought her with you?"

"I had to," he said. Priscilla Andrews made him feel as defensive as his dad usually did. "I didn't want to miss the first team meeting. My new boss is a real hard-ass who wouldn't like that."

She lifted her nose in the air, obviously offended as well as disapproving. "You arranged this practice," she reminded him.

"Tryouts," he corrected her. "I need to start putting my team together."

"You can't just call up the kids you want," she said. "As athletic director, it's my job to post the tryout day and publish it in the school newsletter so everyone who's interested can come out."

He'd stepped on her toes again. But he suspected that wasn't the only thing she was mad about. She confirmed his suspicion when she continued, "And your new boss would prefer that you didn't bring an infant to an ice rink."

"I couldn't find anyone to watch her," he said with frustration. "My dad got a call from Dispatch and had to go into the office. And the boys are here."

"You shouldn't have left her with the boys, anyway." Her eyes were wide with horror. "Please, don't ever leave her with your brothers," she beseeched him.

He laughed at her overreaction. "Hey, I know they're

young. But I was watching them when I was about their age. And we all know I was no angel." Despite some of the daredevil stunts he'd pulled, he hadn't been as wild as some of the kids in their class because Coach Cook had had a very strict policy about no drinking or smoking. Anyone caught partying was suspended—permanently—from his team, no matter how well he played.

That was why Brooks wasn't as worried about his brothers as their father and apparently Priscilla were. "Sheesh, you act like they're psychopaths in training or something. It's not like they drown kittens or anything."

"They killed the fish in the science department."

"Really?" He tightened his hold, albeit gently, on the baby. "Do you have proof?"

"No." Anger flashed in her eyes. "The evidence is gone. They ate them."

"Since the evidence is gone, you have no proof that it was my brothers." Maybe she just hated Hoovers.

"Now you sound like your father."

"God, no. Take that back."

Her lips curved into a slight smile. "It wasn't an insult," she assured him. "Your father's a good man."

"I didn't think you were a fan," he admitted, "after what he did."

"Going over my head?" She shrugged. "I blame you for that. He's a good man but overprotective of his boys."

Realization dawned, staggering Brooks. His father was like that because he hadn't been able to protect his children from what had hurt them most: their mother's desertion.

"He doesn't make any of you take responsibility for

your actions." She glanced down at the ice, where his brothers were shoving each other around. Then she turned her attention back to him and the baby nestled inside his coat. "It hasn't done you any favors."

"You're calling me irresponsible, too?" he asked, recognizing her words as an insult. She hadn't written the note he'd found in the diaper bag, but she shared its sentiment.

She gestured toward his jacket. "Bringing that baby here has proved it. You should have let the social worker find her a suitable foster home if you can't take care of her yourself."

Brooks gritted his teeth again to hold back another curse. "You had no reason to call social services on us."

"Someone abandoned a baby on your doorstep. Authorities needed to be notified."

"My dad is the sheriff," he reminded her. But he couldn't blame her for not trusting Rex to do the right thing after the strings he'd pulled with the job.

"Would he have called the social worker?" she asked. "About his own grandchild?"

"You don't know that yet. It'll take a while for the DNA results to come back."

A lot longer than portrayed on all the popular television programs. Weeks, maybe. But he wouldn't admit that to Priscilla. Instead he glanced down at the squirming baby. "She's my daughter."

"Even if that's proved to be true, it doesn't mean you're the best person to take care of her," she said.

"So just like you don't think I'm qualified for coaching, you don't think I'm qualified for fatherhood, either?"

She held his gaze, hers steady and almost sympathetic. "Do you?"

No. He was pretty damn certain he wasn't cut out for either position. At least, the old Brooks wouldn't have been. But thanks to the concussion, the old Brooks might be gone. He had no idea who or what the new version would be—if he was forced to sit out more than one season.

"I'll figure it out," he assured her—and himself.

"Since you're so convinced she's yours, what's her name?" she asked.

"I wish I knew," he admitted, shifting the baby so she pressed against his heart.

"You really need to give her one."

"I'm sure she has one. And when her mom comes back—" or his father tracked her down "—I'll find out what it is."

"What if she doesn't come back?"

His heart kicked against his ribs. Then he'd be solely responsible for this child. He wouldn't just be babysitting until her mother was found. "I don't know. I don't want to give her a name she'll grow up hating me for."

"Will she grow up with *you* hating *her?*"

Brooks gently tightened his hold on the baby. "What do you mean?"

"If you're her father…will you grow to resent her?" He noted the doubt in her voice.

"Of course not. Why would I do that?"

"Because she'll change your life."

The concussion that had knocked him off the ice and back to Trout Creek had made the biggest difference.

Having a baby left on his doorstep had only changed his life a little more. *Okay, maybe a lot more.*

"Hey, Coach," Ryan called out with a snarky chuckle. "You're wasting your time with Miss Pr— Miss Andrews. The assistant principal isn't your type."

"Yeah, I'm not easy," Priscilla murmured, so quietly that Brooks barely heard her.

"You're too uptight to ever be considered easy," he agreed, earning himself a glare from her green eyes.

The kids were all staring up at them. Ryan pulled off his helmet. "Damn it, Brooks. We need your help down here. We suck!"

He couldn't argue about that, but he warned his brother, "Watch your mouth!"

"They need you down there," Priscilla said. "You can't coach and take care of an infant." Her voice was soft, almost as if she had an ounce of compassion for him. Or maybe she just felt sorry for the baby, since she didn't think he could care for her on his own.

"So you'll look after her until tryouts are over?" he asked, as if he'd mistaken her remark as an offer to help.

"I—I can't watch her," she said, her voice rising with panic.

"It's Saturday," he reminded her, "so it's not like you need to be at school. And you don't need to be here. What made you come?" In addition to the heavy jacket, she wore gloves and earmuffs; she had dressed more for the Icehouse than the warm autumn weather. "You were checking up on me?"

She nodded. "It's my job to make sure you're doing

yours. Even though it wasn't my idea to hire you, I'm responsible for you and for the safety of the kids on your team."

"What—you thought I'd have them drinking and smoking already, me being such a bad influence and all?" He glanced down at her empty hands. "You forgot your camera. You should have brought one to collect evidence to get me fired."

Her lips tightened into their characteristic line of disapproval. But instead of amusing him the way it had at his job interview, it challenged him. Could he get that mouth to relax into a smile? Or to kiss him back?

Where the hell had that thought come from? That concussion had done more damage than he wanted to admit.

"I also came by to inform you that this is not the official tryout. We need to pick another date and start figuring out the practice schedule. Some of these kids— including your brothers—are on the football team, so they can't have conflicting practices. And they have to have time to study."

He hadn't considered that. "Okay, we can talk about scheduling this stuff."

"Not now." She shook her head. "You can't keep her here. If she gets too cold, she'll get sick and…" The faint color in Priscilla's face faded, and her eyes widened with concern.

"She's fine," he assured her. The tiny body was surprisingly warm and cuddly. "Hell, she's keeping me warm."

"She can't stay here."

"I know. And I won't bring her again. I thought Buzz

would have the heaters on, but he said he only runs the blowers during games." He wouldn't be able to bring her to a game, either. "I need to find someone to baby-sit."

She shook her head. "Not me. You should just go home."

"And leave those guys alone?" he asked, shaking his own head. The way they kept shoving each other around, someone was going to get hurt.

"Then send them home, too."

"I can't do that," he said, then pitched his voice lower. "I need to work with them every minute I can." He had to build a good team, a strong team—a winning team. He couldn't step in for his childhood idol and fail. "If you watch her this one time," he coaxed, "I promise I'll find a babysitter. It'll just be for an hour or so. I'll pick her up at your house."

She shook her head fiercely. "Really. I can't."

"I wasn't ready for this," he admitted, his pride be damned. "I had no idea I had a child. But just because I don't know how to be a father yet doesn't mean I'm going to be a bad one. I just need time. And a little bit of help." He pulled the baby from the warmth of his flannel-lined jacket and held her out to Priscilla.

She stared down at the child with that mixture of dread, fear and longing. The baby met her gaze with round, unblinking eyes. "You—you don't want me to watch her," she stammered.

"Yes, I do."

"But she's so tiny. So *fragile*."

"You'll do fine." Hell, she couldn't do any worse

than he was. His room was trashed—full of baby stuff, the sheets stripped off his mattress. He hadn't been able to find clean ones to replace them. Not that he would have gotten any sleep, anyway. Nothing he'd tried— rocking, walking, even singing—had soothed the baby. Of course, he sang so badly it had probably only made her cry harder.

He watched Priscilla's delicate throat as she swallowed hard. Her eyes stayed wide, though, full of that fear he was dying to ask about. But he held back his questions—and his breath—until she slid her hands around the infant and clasped her close to her body.

"Just for a little while," she specified.

"I'm not going to leave her with you," he assured her. The child had already been abandoned once. No matter how scared Brooks was that he knew nothing about being a good father, he could learn.

Would Priscilla give him enough time before she called the social worker again? Or would she pick up her cell the minute she left and report him for bringing the baby to the arena?

He opened his mouth to call her back, but the shouts on the ice would have drowned out his voice.

"Coach!"

"Coach!"

All morning his brothers had been calling him that, too, even though he had yet to earn the title.

"I'm coming down," he assured them. Not that it would do any good. He had been a team captain in high school, college and the NHL. But he had never been a coach. Priscilla was right; he wasn't qualified for the job.

"You coming out on the ice with us?" one of the boys asked, his eyes wide with awe.

Brooks shook his head. It still pounded with a dull ache. "I didn't bring my skates."

"He brought a baby instead," another boy griped with a snort of disgust. "My dad's right. Hoover's a has-been—" The words barely left his lips before Ryan slammed him down on the ice.

"Take it back!" the teenager warned his teammate.

Brooks flinched, remembering his last fight and the repercussions from it. He'd ended up losing what had mattered most to him. He rushed down to the boards. "Break it up, guys! Ryan, help him up."

While Ryan dragged the smaller kid to his feet, Brad skated up to defend his oldest brother. "Wes, your dad's a worthless drunk who's never left Trout Creek except to go to the county lockup. He's a *never* been."

The kid broke free of Ryan's grasp and shoved his gloves into Brad's chest, knocking him on his butt. Brad's breath escaped in a loud curse.

"C'mon, guys," Brooks said. "Quit the fighting. You have got to learn to work together, not against each other. What the hell's the matter with you?"

"We suck!" Ryan wailed.

Brooks nodded. "Yeah, you do." He knew from having coffee at the Trout Creek Inn the other day that the school hadn't had a winning team in a while, but the players couldn't have been this bad. "We don't have enough kids yet. Did you lose a bunch of seniors?"

"We lost our goalie and a defenseman," Brad said.

"They graduated?" That explained the holes in the

team. His father had picked a great time to talk him into coaching—during a restructuring year.

Ryan shook his head. "They didn't graduate. Miss Priss suspended them."

"Why did she suspend them? If it was over drinking, I support her decision. And I'll do the same thing," he warned them. "We're going to follow Coach Cook's rules."

"What are *your* rules?" Wes asked. "Do as I say, not as I do?"

The kid was a jerk, but his remark was fair. "I've done some stupid things off the ice," Brooks admitted. Like some of the print ads and commercials his sports agent had talked him into, back when he'd been the fresh new star of the NHL. Right now, being back in the first arena he'd ever played in, that life felt like a dream—both good and bad. "But when I play, I'm serious. Focused. I want you all to do the same."

"Those players wouldn't have broken Coach Cook's rules." Brad was defending them even though he hadn't been on the team at the time.

"Then why were they suspended?"

Ryan snorted. "Grades, which is total crap. Miss Priss is just looking for reasons to bust up every sports team. She hates athletes."

"Is that what she was doing here?" Brad asked. "Getting ready to suspend more players? Or was she… Did she tell you about something else?" The fourteen-year-old glanced toward Ryan with the same guilty expression he'd worn the night before.

"What did you guys do to Miss Andrews?" Brooks

asked. "And don't BS me. I can tell you pulled something."

Wes ratted them out with a vengeful smirk. "They TP'd her place."

"Hey, you helped," Ryan reminded him.

Brooks sighed. "Why?"

"We didn't think she hired you," Brad admitted. "It's like she's out to get us—suspending players, not hiring a coach."

"You have a coach—me." Such as he was.

"But she told me on the bus back from the football game that she didn't hire you," Brad protested.

"It doesn't matter who hired me," Brooks hedged, even though he knew it mattered to Priscilla.

"Yeah, it does," Brad argued. "She's out to get us."

"I doubt that's true," Brooks reasoned, though he wasn't so sure himself. "You said the players were suspended for bad grades."

Brad snorted. "Debbie? I doubt it."

"Who's Debbie?"

"Our goalie," Ryan said.

Brooks wasn't a chauvinist, but he had definitely played with and for a bunch. "You had a female goalie?"

"Hey, she didn't play like a girl," Ryan said in her defense. He jerked a glove toward the current goalie. "Adam's the one who plays like a girl."

Brooks couldn't argue that, and neither did the stand-in goalie. "Coach Cook let a girl play? Really?" The old man must have mellowed after Brooks had graduated.

"Debbie's his granddaughter," Brad explained. "So

you don't know why Miss Andrews suspended her from the team? She probably did it just to get Adam off the bench."

"Adam?" Brooks glanced at the goalie again.

"She's my aunt," he explained. "But, hey, I don't want to be in the net. I'm better out on the ice."

"Miss Priss is a bitch," Ryan said, then spat on the ice. "She likes causing trouble."

"That's the same thing she says about you." Brooks grimaced as the dull pounding in his head intensified. "And unfortunately, you've proved her right."

"C'mon, Brooks—it's just TPing," Ryan said with a grimace. "You can't say you've never done it."

No, he couldn't say that—not without lying through his teeth. "Practice is over," he said, clapping his cold hands together. "We're going over to Miss Andrews's house to clean up."

"Wh-what? All of us?" Wes asked.

"You helped," Brooks reminded him. "Everybody, go to the locker room and change back into your street clothes."

He couldn't wait to get to Priscilla's place—to make sure his child was still there and Priscilla was okay. When she'd stared down at his daughter, she'd looked nearly as scared as his dad had when Brooks had awakened from that coma.

There'd been more to her look than just being nervous around babies. He'd seen pain as well as fear. And Brooks wanted to know why.

Chapter Six

"Did you hear that?" Priscilla asked as she pulled the phone away from the baby's face and held it to her own ear again. "Can you hear her breathing? Does it sound like she's breathing harder? Is there a rattle?"

"She's just sighing," the school nurse responded. "She sounds content and healthy. But of course, I shouldn't be making that evaluation over the phone."

"No," Priscilla agreed. "You need to come over here." She shouldn't be alone with the baby; she never should have taken her in the first place. "I think she's going to get a cold. She was in the arena for at least a half hour." And that was the only reason Priscilla had kept the baby, to get her out of the Icehouse and warm her up. Because a cold could turn into something else, something dangerous.

Priscilla's breath caught in her lungs and an ache filled her. A cold could lead to loss. And so much pain.

"Babies have a strong immune system. I'm sure she's fine. Does she have a fever?"

"I don't have a thermometer," Priscilla said. For her own sanity, she'd had to get rid of all the baby things.

She'd brought only her own clothes and books with her to Trout Creek.

"Just touch her. See if she feels hot."

Priscilla reached trembling fingers toward the baby, who was lying in the center of her queen-sized sleigh bed. The infant was too weak to roll over and fall off the side. But Priscilla still hadn't dared leave her alone. She'd made that mistake once before.

Brooks shouldn't have trusted her with the child. Really, Priscilla should have called the social worker and reported him for bringing a baby to a cold arena. Instead, she'd called Trudy, the school nurse. She brushed her fingertips across the soft forehead of the sleeping child. "She doesn't seem too warm."

But neither had her baby, until she'd started burning up. Then it had been too late, the meningitis too advanced for the antibiotics to work. And her eight-week-old baby girl had died.

Tears stung her eyes, but Priscilla blinked them back. She'd been numb for so long, but touching this baby, Brooks's baby, had thawed something inside her. She continued to stroke her fingers across the baby's soft forehead and over the fuzz of dark hair. She was so beautiful, so perfect, just like Courtney had been, with her little bald head and bright blue eyes. Priscilla couldn't fight the tears anymore as they began to stream down her face.

"Miss Andrews, are you all right?" Trudy asked.

She sucked in a deep, steadying breath. "Yes. Yes, I'm fine," she lied. "I'm sorry for calling you."

"It's all right," Trudy assured her. "If Mr. Hoover

needs anything, I'd be happy to help him out. Is it true that he doesn't know who the mother is—that she just left the baby on his doorstep?"

Unwilling to exchange gossip for medical advice, Priscilla lied again. "I don't know, but thanks for your help."

She'd no more than clicked the off button than the phone rang again. "Trudy, sorry for hanging up on you," she said. Her mother would have given her such a lecture for her lack of manners.

"Trudy?" a woman asked. "This is Margaret Everly. Is this Priscilla Andrews?"

"Yes, it is."

"I wanted to thank you, Miss Andrews, for reporting the Hoover baby situation to me."

Since the social worker had already done that in the message she'd left the previous evening, Priscilla suspected there was more to this call. "You don't know for certain that she's a Hoover, do you?"

"The DNA results won't be back for a while," the social worker replied. "But a preliminary blood test couldn't rule out Brooks Hoover as the baby's father."

"What does that mean?"

"The Hoovers told me last night that I can share this information with you, otherwise I wouldn't be able to violate their privacy," Mrs. Everly said. "Brooks and the baby have the same blood type and several of the same markers."

"So that's why you let him take her home?" But Brooks had been certain the baby was his, even before they'd gone to the hospital. How had he known?

It wasn't as if he'd carried the child for nine months. Hell, he hadn't even known he'd gotten the mother pregnant. But when he'd found the baby on his doorstep, it was as if he'd recognized her, as if he'd instinctively known she was his. And he'd authorized Mrs. Everly to release the blood test results to Priscilla because he'd wanted her to know, too.

So she wouldn't worry or just to prove his point? Settling onto the bed next to the baby, Priscilla studied her face, and she could see it now—the Hoover look. It was there in the dimple in her cheek, in the fists curled at her sides as she slept.

"I also let them take her because the sheriff has a foster care license," Mrs. Everly explained. "He got it years ago in case there was a situation where he had to care for a child until legal guardians could be located."

Priscilla nodded even though the woman couldn't see her. "I appreciate your calling to explain that."

"That's not why I phoned," the woman admitted. "I have a favor to ask of you."

"A favor?"

"Yes, I'm going to be busy with home visits on the other side of the county this week, so I won't be able to get out to Trout Creek myself until later next week," Mrs. Everly explained. "I could really use your help, Miss Andrews, and I thought, given that you had called me with your concerns, you might want to check in on them for your peace of mind and mine."

"You want me to spy on the Hoovers for you?" Brooks already thought she was doing that because she'd shown up at the practice he shouldn't have called.

"It wouldn't be spying," Mrs. Everly insisted. "You'd just be checking on the welfare of a child."

"I'm not the right person for this job," Priscilla said. She hadn't been able to ensure the welfare of her own child.

"I need your help," the social worker pressed. "Other people might be intimidated by the sheriff or dazzled by Brooks Hoover's celebrity, but I know you'll be objective, given the situation."

She had just called the nurse over the baby's sigh. She couldn't be objective and she couldn't get involved. Just sitting here next to the sleeping infant brought back too many memories and too much pain.

"I—I don't know," Priscilla said.

"You're not worried any longer that they might not be able to properly care for her?" the older woman asked.

During the five years she'd been assistant principal at Trout Creek High, Priscilla had met with the social worker about certain students. Those kids had been teenagers, old enough to tell her about their problems. The infant lying on the bed could not express herself. She needed someone to speak for her.

And Brooks couldn't be trusted to protect her the way babies needed to be protected. "Yes."

"So you'll do it?"

"Yes." And just as she'd hung up on the nurse, she hung up on the social worker.

"Hey, everything okay?" a deep voice asked from the doorway.

Priscilla blinked back the tears that had welled in her eyes and turned toward the man who'd invaded her bedroom. "What are you doing here?"

"We wrapped up early. The kids had something else they needed to do."

"See, that's why we have to coordinate these things," Priscilla said as she rose from the bed. Not wanting him to notice the tearstains on her face, she turned toward the window. "You can't just call them at the last minute."

"They're not at another practice," he said.

A movement in the yard distracted her. She might have thought it was a deer, if not for the bright clothing. She leaned closer to the glass. A teenager jumped up and down, pulling tissue from tree limbs. Then she noticed other kids doing the same.

"They're cleaning up," Brooks said, his deep voice close to her ear. He'd crossed the room and stood behind her, his chest brushing against her back as he stared out the window, too.

Goose bumps lifted on her skin, and she shivered at his nearness. "You persuaded them to do that?"

The kids pulled down every tissue-paper streamer from the tree branches, where they had been strung like Christmas lights. She would never have managed to get the kids to admit to TPing her place, let alone clean up their mess. Maybe she had misjudged Brooks Hoover.

But then she remembered her real question. "What are you doing here?" she asked again. "In my bedroom?"

STARING AT THE CARVED OAK bed with frilly white sheets that matched the frilly white curtains, Brooks realized exactly where he was. "Uh…you didn't answer when I knocked, but your car was here. I wanted to make sure everything was all right."

"She's fine!"

The defensive tone of her voice drew his attention, but Priscilla wouldn't meet his gaze.

"She fell asleep on the way here and hasn't woken up," she continued, "even when I took her out of the car seat and changed her."

Brooks chuckled. "I'm not surprised."

"Why? Does she sleep a lot? Do you think she's sick?"

"No." He grinned. "In fact, she didn't sleep at all last night. So it's no wonder she's out now." He groaned. "And since she's sleeping today, she'll be sure to stay up all night again."

Priscilla expelled a little sigh of relief. "That's good."

"That I'm up all night?"

"That she's okay."

"The doctor who checked her out at the hospital last night said she was very healthy," he assured her.

"Oh, that's good—really good."

"You're the one I wanted to make sure was all right," he said. "You seemed a little nervous about watching her. And you look pretty upset right now."

Her eyes were shiny. Tears? And her cheeks looked damp, too. "You've been crying," he said.

She shook her head.

"You were on the phone. That must've been why you didn't hear me knock. Did that call upset you?" A protective instinct made Brooks want to strike whoever had hurt her—which was funny, since he'd probably hurt her himself years ago, when he used to tease her.

She shook her head again. "I'm fine."

But she still wouldn't meet his gaze. So he closed his hands around her shoulders and turned her to face him.

"You're not fine," he said. But, physically, she was. Even with tear-reddened skin, she was beautiful, those deep green eyes softened with vulnerability. "Tell me what's wrong."

Her mouth curved slightly into a faint smile. "Why? What are you going to do about it?"

Quit? It was probably what she wanted—if that's what had upset her. But he suspected she was too tough to cry over the fact he'd been hired. No, whatever had brought her to tears was very painful, probably too painful for her to share with a man she did not trust. So all he could do was help make her forget about whatever had hurt her.

"What am I going to do about it?" he asked, moving his hands from her shoulders, down the curve of her back to her waist. He pulled her against his chest. "I'm going to kiss it better."

He waited for her to tense or to shove him away. Instead she laughed. His breath caught at the transformation—the brightness of her eyes and the overwhelming beauty of her full lips curved into a wide smile. And he followed through on his threat and lowered his mouth to hers.

Her breath mingled with his as she gasped in surprise. But then she kissed him back, her lips—so silky soft—pressed against his. And her fingers tangled in his hair, clutching his head close.

He deepened the kiss, touching his tongue to the full curve of her lower lip. He slid the tip across it before slipping it inside her moist, sweet mouth.

She moaned and shifted closer, her breasts soft against his chest. He tightened his grasp on her waist, his hands moving over the curve of her hips. But before he could tug her nearer, someone shouted.

"Coach!"

"Hey, Coach!"

The baby awakened with a startled cry. And Priscilla jerked from his arms and stumbled back. Her eyes dry now, wide with shock, she stared at him. And he suspected he hadn't kissed anything better. If anything, he'd kissed it worse.

He carefully lifted the baby from the bed and carried her into the living room. She settled down before he even crossed the hardwood floor. His brothers stood outside the open door to the front porch. The other kids who'd come along to help lingered on the gravel driveway, hanging back and partially hiding behind their vehicles.

"We're done," Ryan said, his brown eyes hard with resentment.

Brooks suspected that right now they weren't too happy he'd stayed in Trout Creek. "Did you get it all?"

"Every ply," Brad snapped.

"Now you need to apologize to Ms. Andrews," he said, glancing back over his shoulder to where she stood behind him—quite a ways behind him, as if she was afraid he might grab her again. Or that the kids might notice she'd been crying. What the hell had made her cry?

He doubted she would tell him, even if they didn't have an audience. As if eager to get rid of him, she'd brought out the baby carrier, blanket and diaper bag.

"What would we be sorry for?" Brad asked belligerently. "We didn't do anything."

"C'mon," he urged them. "You owe her an apology."

"We agreed to clean up," Brad reminded him. "And that was just so she'd consider lifting Debbie's suspension. We're not going to admit to doing anything."

Ryan shook his head in agreement. "She'll suspend us for sure."

"I haven't picked the team yet," he reminded them. "Neither of you are guaranteed a spot on it."

"But we're your brothers," Ryan whined.

"And we're the best hockey players in Trout Creek," Brad arrogantly added.

At the moment that didn't mean a whole lot.

"You need us," Brad threatened, then grabbed his brother and headed back to the Jeep.

"Smart-ass," Brooks muttered. He turned back to Priscilla. "You're right. We need another tryout."

Her pretty mouth had thinned into that tight look of disapproval again as she handed over the car seat. "And they're right. I would suspend them if they admitted to TPing my trees."

"They still should have apologized." He settled the baby into her carrier and took the blanket and diaper bag from Priscilla's outstretched hand.

"It wouldn't have been sincere. You only got them here with the promise that I'd consider letting Debbie back on the team."

That was what they'd thought, but he'd really wanted them to take responsibility for their actions, the way he was trying to do with the baby. But since Priscilla always thought the worst of him, she probably wouldn't believe that—especially after he'd kissed her.

So instead he asked, "Will you?"

She shook her head. "I can't."

"Are her grades really that bad?" he wondered. "I heard she was a great student."

"You heard she was a great player."

"Yeah," he admitted. "And I need more great players on this team to have any hope of winning a game."

"You need players who want to play," Priscilla said. "And Debbie doesn't want to play."

"Why not?" he asked.

"You really have no idea?"

He shrugged. "No."

"I don't know. But you can't understand how someone might not want to play?"

"No, I can't," he answered honestly. From the moment he'd strapped on his first pair of skates and picked up a stick, it was all he had ever wanted to do.

"So if it was up to you, you'd be playing instead of coaching?"

"Of course." Smelling the ice, watching the kids play—or whatever they'd been doing—had made him want to get back to the sport even more.

Priscilla's gaze slipped to the carrier in his hand. He glanced down at the baby, who had fallen back asleep. Would he be playing—even if he got medical clearance—*now?*

"Thanks for watching her," he said as the pressure weighed down on his chest once more. He felt like that teenager again, helping his single dad raise his younger brothers. Hockey had helped him out of the trap his life had felt like twelve years ago. But it couldn't free him now.

"I won't be doing it again," she said as if warning him. "You'll need to make other arrangements in the future."

When he was cleared to play, and he had to have faith that eventually he would be, he'd have to find someone to watch her. A nanny to travel with him? How the hell else would he manage…*alone?*

The cabin fell eerily silent after they left, quieter than it had ever been. Usually the silence relaxed Priscilla, but this afternoon it left her restless.

Or maybe that was Brooks's fault. Not only had he manipulated her into watching the baby, he'd kissed her. Why? He'd probably just felt sorry for her, since she'd been such an emotional mess.

Damn him.

She'd preferred the numbness she'd felt until now. But holding that infant, watching her sleep, had thawed Priscilla. And his kiss had warmed her up.

She touched her fingers to lips that still tingled from the contact with his. The man knew how to kiss. But then, he'd had plenty of experience back in high school. She couldn't imagine how many women he had kissed since—so many that he didn't even know who the mother of his child was.

Priscilla would not be kissing him again. Overcome with emotion, she'd lost her mind for a minute there. She'd forgotten who she was—his boss.

Pushing the kiss from her mind, she turned on her laptop to focus on work. But instead of going to the school site and updating student files, she went instead to the online social network. And pulled up *his* page.

Her ex-husband's picture downloaded, revealing his reddish-brown hair first. His hairline had receded, just a little. Remembering how he'd often studied it in the mirror, she smiled. But then his eyes appeared, full of warmth and happiness.

She had seen him that happy only once, the day their daughter was born. He hadn't been that happy on their wedding day. Of course, if she hadn't been pregnant, he probably wouldn't have married her. They had always been more friends than lovers. And after Courtney had died, they hadn't even been able to maintain the friendship.

He wasn't alone in the photograph. His wife, a beautiful woman with light-colored hair, sat next to him. And each of them held a child: one a few years old and the other a toddler.

Priscilla wanted to be happy for him. After all, she had loved him. But all she felt now was bitterness and pain.

With his picture-perfect new family, he had moved on; she had just moved back to Trout Creek. Maybe Maureen was right. Maybe it was time Priscilla truly put the past behind her, instead of just trying to forget it.

That hadn't worked, anyway. While she'd dated a few times since coming home, she hadn't really given anyone a chance. She had never kissed anyone the way she had Brooks Hoover—maybe not even her husband.

Chapter Seven

"Aren't you going to watch the game?" Brad asked as he tromped into the kitchen.

Brooks glanced over his shoulder at his youngest brother and shook his head. "No."

"But it's your team—the Eagles. Don't you want to see how they do?"

Without him? No. He was afraid they might do well, that they might not need him. Maybe they wouldn't call him back, even when he got his medical clearance.

"It's just an exhibition game," he said. The regular season wouldn't start for weeks yet. "And I've got my hands full here." Literally.

"You're doing dishes?" Brad asked, his voice full of shock and disgust.

Since he'd been back, his father wasn't the only Hoover that Brooks had disappointed. His brothers had expected more from him—more than he was. They wanted him to be the man he was on the ice—the relentless, aggressive player who never made a wrong move. Off the ice, he didn't seem to be making any right ones.

"I'm not doing the dishes." Brooks stood at the sink, the spray nozzle in one hand, the infant in the other as water sluiced over her. He held her carefully, her body resting on the towel he'd used to cover the cold stainless steel. Those big, dark eyes of hers stared up at him, studying him, as if she didn't completely trust him not to drown her. He wasn't so confident himself. But he couldn't ask his dad to give her every bath. And taking care of her got his mind off another female.

"You're giving the kid a bath in the sink?" Brad sounded horrified.

"Have you seen the tub?" he asked. It wasn't that dirty, but when he'd leaned over it, he'd gotten dizzy. The effects of the concussion had yet to wear off.

Maybe that was why he'd kissed Priscilla Andrews the day before, because the concussion had addled his brain. Even though she was beautiful, she wasn't his type. She was too serious and too vulnerable. Already wounded, she would get hurt even more if she got involved with him. But hell, she was too smart to be interested in him. She had kissed him back, though. The memory of her silky lips would have kept him awake even if the baby hadn't.

He shook his head and pushed the kiss from his mind.

"Somebody should do these dishes," Brooks said, gesturing toward the dirty pile he'd taken from the sink and stacked on the counter.

"Myrtle comes tomorrow," Brad said.

"What about Myrtle?" their dad asked as he joined them in the kitchen. He pulled open the refrigerator door and snagged a beer.

Brad smirked. "Just talking about her cleaning. Hey, I'll take one of those." He gestured toward the brown bottle.

"Try it and I'll arrest you myself," the sheriff warned.

"Hey, you're all missing the game," Ryan called, sticking his head through the doorway between the kitchen and family room.

They would probably hassle Brooks until he joined them, so he focused on finishing this bath. But the baby squirmed. To make sure he didn't drop her, he tossed down the sprayer to hold her with both hands. Water shot over his face and shirt and across the room behind him.

"Hey!" Brad protested, while their dad laughed.

"You're washing the kid again?" Ryan asked. "What are you feeding her? Turbo lax?"

Brad sputtered as he wiped water from his face. "Gross!"

"She wasn't dirty," Brooks assured them.

"Then why give her a bath?" Ryan asked.

"He doesn't know what he's doing," Brad explained, as if Brooks wasn't even there. "He shouldn't be wasting his time trying to take care of a baby."

"Wasting his time?" their father asked. "You think raising kids is a waste of time?"

"Not *you* raising kids," Brad said, looking embarrassed. "But Brooks..."

"He's got other things he should be doing," Ryan added. "Like playing."

"What about coaching?" Brooks asked. "Don't you want me as your coach?"

Brad chuckled. "Not unless you guarantee us spots on the team."

"You'll be lucky if I even let you try out," he teased. He lifted the naked baby from the sink and wrapped her in a dry towel.

"When are the official tryouts?" Ryan asked.

He shrugged. "Whenever Ms. Andrews says they are." He wouldn't step on her toes again. In fact, he would try to avoid her from now on. With the baby and coaching and the concussion, he had more than enough things on his mind. He needed to stop thinking about her, stop dreaming about her, stop wanting her.

PRISCILLA RAPPED HER knuckles against the door to the nurse's office. "Just a moment," Trudy called out.

She could have just phoned the woman, Priscilla thought; she really only had to check if the flu and meningitis vaccines had arrived before she sent out a memo in the school newsletter. But she'd also wanted to talk to Trudy about her anxious call over the weekend. Ever since she'd returned to Trout Creek, she'd been careful to avoid being the subject of town gossip. So she'd hate it if her panic about the baby became known.

Finally the door opened and a teenage girl stepped into the hall, which was deserted, since first hour had already begun.

"Debbie." Priscilla greeted her with a mixture of relief and concern. The teenager had missed a lot of school at the end of last year and the beginning of this one. "Are you all right?"

The dark-haired girl nodded, but she wouldn't lift her head to meet Priscilla's eyes. "Yeah, yeah…"

When she tried to step around her, Priscilla caught her arm. "I'd like to talk to you."

"Miss Andrews?" Trudy asked. The older woman stepped into the hall, too. "You wanted to see me?"

"Yes, but I'd really like to talk to Debbie for a minute first. Can we use your office?"

"Sure. I need to get a cup of coffee from the lounge. Do you want me to bring you anything? Herbal tea?"

No doubt after Priscilla's hysterical phone call, the nurse didn't think she should have any caffeine. "No, thanks."

"I really need to get to class," Debbie said. "I'm already late."

"Yes, you are," Priscilla pointed out as she held open the door. "So a couple minutes more won't matter."

With a resigned shrug, Debbie stepped back inside the nurse's office. The small room held a locked cabinet, a desk and a couch on which kids could rest until they felt better or their parents picked them up. Her breath hitched when Priscilla closed the door.

"I'm all right, really," the girl insisted. But when she lifted her head, her eyes were red and swollen.

Recognizing the girl's pain, Priscilla reached out and patted her shoulder. At sixteen, Debbie was already taller than her, and had the wide shoulders and strength of the male athletes with whom she'd played hockey. But no matter how tough she was, there were things a teenage girl just couldn't handle on her own.

"How's your grandfather doing?" Priscilla asked. She couldn't imagine how the girl had felt when the only father figure she'd known had had a stroke. Coach

Cook had always been so strong, but the stroke had nearly killed him.

"He's getting better," Debbie replied. "He's home now."

"That's good. It'll save your mom and you the long drive to the rehab center to visit him."

She nodded. "But Mom still has to drive him into the city for his physical and speech therapy." Which must leave the girl on her own quite a bit.

"That must be hard on your mom."

Debbie nodded. "But everyone's been pitching in. We got, like, a dozen casseroles in the fridge. Somebody's always bringing over food, or mowing the yard or chopping wood."

That was part of the reason Priscilla had moved back to Trout Creek. After living in a big, impersonal city, she appreciated the caring community in which she'd grown up.

"But Mom can't work all her shifts at the store," Debbie continued. "So I've been picking up some of them."

"Is that why you've been missing so much school? You've been working instead?" There were state rules regarding how many hours a minor could work. If the Cooks were having financial difficulties, Priscilla didn't want to have to enforce them, but neither did she want Debbie's education to suffer. The girl looked exhausted.

She shook her head. "No, I've been sick a lot."

"So your mother said when she called in your absences."

"You think she's lying for me?" Debbie asked, her voice defensive.

"No, your mother wouldn't lie for you. I just hope you're not getting run-down, that you're not doing too much."

"I'm only working as many hours as I'm allowed. And I'm feeling better now, so I won't be missing any more school."

"That's good. I'm glad you're feeling better." And maybe she was physically, but Priscilla recognized the girl's emotional pain and exhaustion. "If you ever need anything, I hope you know you can come to me. I'm here for you…even if you just want to talk."

Debbie nodded again, but tears welled in her eyes. "Everything's better now."

"Hey, Mrs. K.," a male voice called out.

Debbie gasped, her eyes wide as she stared at the turning knob. The door opened, and Brad Hoover barged into the room.

"Oh, sorry," he said. "I was looking for the nurse. Hey, Debbie, are you going to try out for the team again?"

She shook her head.

"But your grades can't be that bad. You're all honors."

"Not anymore," she said as she pushed past him and fled from the room.

"What's her problem?" he asked with an accusatory look at Priscilla.

"What's *your* problem, Mr. Hoover?" Trudy walked into her office, a steaming cup of coffee in her hand. "You're not going to sweet-talk me into letting you cut class, young man. Not like your brother used to."

"Ryan?" Brad asked in surprise.

"Brooks," she replied, with a smile and a wink at Priscilla. "I've been around a long time."

"Yeah," he agreed. "But I just got a question. Can you get hepatitis from being around baby crap? All Brooks's kid does is spew all over the place. It's gross. I can't believe he's keeping her."

"He's keeping her?" Trudy asked.

"Yeah, he thinks he's gotta. That it's his obligation or something."

Obligation. Priscilla winced. She could identify with the poor baby girl. Obligation had put a ring on her finger, had made a man try to love her. She'd deserved more than that pathetic attempt. She deserved a man who could love her with his whole heart. And that little girl deserved a father who would love her the same way.

And Priscilla doubted the selfish boy she'd known had grown up enough to love like that.

USING HIS BACK, Brooks pushed open the door to the Trout Creek Inn. All conversation ceased as he stepped inside the restaurant with the baby swinging in her carrier from his right hand. In the left, he held the strap to her diaper bag, which had slipped from his shoulder.

How did mothers manage all this crap? How had his father?

A plate dropped, and half an English muffin rolled across the scarred pine floor. He stopped it with his foot and then glanced up. "Hey, everyone."

"Well, I'll be damned—it's true," an elderly man announced with a chuckle. "He's got a baby." The old man's cronies sat with him at a corner table, a walker and a cane leaning against the paneled wall beside them.

"Brooks Hoover, what the hell are you doing with a baby?" Mr. Faulkner asked. The mayor sat at the big round table in the middle of the inn's dining room. Brooks's dad sat on one side of him; Buzz, the owner of the Trout Creek Icehouse, sat on the other. The round table had always held the town's movers and shakers, the council members, the business owners, the mayor and the sheriff.

"She's my daughter," Brooks replied, causing another break in conversation. He repeated it louder for the old fogies with the hearing aids. "She's my daughter."

The mayor turned to his old friend and slapped him on the back. "Well, congratulations, Gramps."

His comment inspired a flurry of congratulations. A redheaded waitress who looked vaguely familiar to Brooks gave him a hug. She wrapped her arms around his neck and squeezed.

And over her shoulder, he met Priscilla's gaze. She sat at a corner booth with her boss. Mr. Drover, looking about a hundred with his skeletal build and thinning white hair, weakly lifted his mug in greeting. Priscilla continued to stare at Brooks, her green eyes unfathomable.

Had she thought about their kiss as much as he had these past few days?

"Is it true?" the waitress asked, still gripping him. "The baby has no mother?"

He shook his head. "She does." Just as he had a mother. The woman had to be out there somewhere.

"But you're not married?"

He shook his head again, and though his hands were occupied, tried easing away from the clingy woman. He remembered who she was. She'd been a couple of years behind him in school. "But you are, Brenda, last I heard."

She shrugged. "Randy drives a truck. He's never around."

"Well, I'm not sure how long *I'll* be around." He finally shook her off and slid into the chair Buzz had pulled out for him.

"The Eagles needed you at the game the other day," he said. "They got their asses kicked nearly as badly as the high school team these past few years."

"See, that's why Trout Creek needs him as a coach right now," his father said. "We have to get the team back to what it once was."

"He'd probably have to play, for that to happen," the mayor remarked. "Though I heard your younger boys show some promise."

"They do," Brooks agreed. "I just have to get them some teammates." But he hadn't been able to track down Priscilla to approve the hockey schedule. Even when she was at the school, she'd been too busy to see him.

"You think you can do what Coach Cook hasn't managed in years?" Buzz asked. "You think you can put together a winning team?"

His breath caught as that pressure returned to his chest. "I can't make any promises." He glanced up and caught Priscilla's gaze again. She probably wasn't within hearing distance now that other conversations had resumed, but it didn't matter. She already knew that about him.

"They asked your coach about you during that

game," the mayor remarked. "He didn't say anything about you not being cleared to play."

"But he's not," his dad answered for him, the color fading from his face. "He can't…."

"You look fine—what'd you hurt?" Buzz asked.

Brooks set the carrier on the floor and rocked it with his foot so the baby would stay asleep. Then he tapped his fingers to his forehead. "Hit my head. But it's hard."

His dad snorted.

"I'll be playing again." He had to, because he didn't have a whole lot of hope this coaching thing would work out, especially since he couldn't even get the athletic director to talk to him.

His dad didn't snort this time, just tensed his jaw.

"What will you do with that little pink bundle?" a woman asked as she walked up to the round table. Except for the lines around her eyes, Myrtle didn't look her age, which must have hovered around fifty. Brooks had gone to school with her kids, whom she'd raised on her own after her husband died. Her slim, delicate build belied an inner toughness. The petite blonde crouched next to the car seat and ran a finger along the baby's cheek. The kid opened her mouth and a bubble slipped out.

"Hey, Myrtle," Brooks said in greeting, ignoring the question.

"Hey, honey, it's good to have you back home." She slid an arm around his shoulders and dropped a kiss on the top of his head, as if she knew where he'd been injured, though she couldn't have heard him tell his dad's friends. Even during the interview after the exhibition game the other night, no one had reported what had happened to him during that unfortunate practice. And, not wanting to worry the younger boys, their father hadn't told anyone how seriously Brooks had been hurt. Yet Myrtle seemed to know.

She unclasped the baby from the car seat and lifted her in her arms. Then she dropped into the chair next to his dad and gave him a wink. "She's definitely a Hoover, a heartbreaker in the making."

"Get Myrtle some coffee and get the boy a cup, too," the mayor directed the waitress, who hovered near their table. "He looks like hell."

Brooks blinked his gritty eyes and pushed a hand through his messy hair. "She doesn't sleep much."

"I don't blame her—poor thing, living with a bunch of men," Myrtle said as she swayed, rocking the infant in her arms. "You need some live-in help."

"There's barely room enough for all of us in that house," his father replied. "But we definitely need some help."

Myrtle slid the fingertips of her free hand across the back of his dad's. "I'll come by more often."

Brooks couldn't believe his eyes. His father was blushing! Was the town cleaning lady the woman Rex was seeing? Brooks had been as self-absorbed as that note with the baby had said. Over the years he'd never really asked about his dad's life. Hell, he hadn't figured Rex had much of a life, between raising his brothers and providing law and order in Trout Creek.

"Other women will be willing to help out," the waitress said as she turned over the cup in front of Brooks and filled it. Her breasts brushed against his shoulder, and she shot him a sideways look of invitation.

A married woman? No way in hell was he interested. He glanced over to see Priscilla get up from the booth and head toward the door. She wore one of those drab suits again, a loose jacket and a skirt just short enough to reveal her sleek calves but not a hint of her knees or thighs.

He pushed back his chair and eased around the waitress. "I'll be right back," he said. "Hey, Priscilla!"

She didn't stop, just kept walking out the door and across the lot to her vehicle. He lengthened his stride to catch her, closing his hand around hers as she reached for the door handle. "Hey..."

She drew in an audible breath, then looked up at him. "Hello."

"Why didn't you stop?"

"I didn't hear you," she said, but he could tell it was a lie.

"Was I supposed to use your last name again? Are we back to formalities?" After that kiss and all the things he'd imagined doing to her since? The baby wasn't the only one who'd kept him awake.

"No."

"Why are you avoiding me?"

Her cheeks grew pink, and not from the brisk morning breeze, he was quite sure. She jerked her hand out from beneath his. "I've been busy. I need to get to the school now—before the bell rings."

"I don't think you'll be marked tardy," he teased, leaning closer to her. The wind blew her hair across her face, so that it tangled with her long lashes. He reached out and pulled the strands away from her eyes.

Her pupils widened, swallowing the green irises. And she licked her lips. "I—I really need to be at school."

"And so do I," he said. "I need an office, somewhere I can meet with kids and strategize how I'm going to coach this team." He required more than space to figure that out, though. "Do you have a place I can use?"

She shrugged. "I might be able to find you something."

"And we need to set a date for tryouts and get practices started."

She sighed. "Yes."

"I've been trying for the past few days to talk to you, but the secretary claims you're busy."

"I am."

"You're not just pissed because I got this job, and you don't want me to have it?"

"I'm not that petty."

But her cheeks reddened even more, and dread hit his stomach as he figured out what she'd been busy doing. He thought he'd recognized one of the men who'd been waiting in the office to see her the other day. The old guy had been a hockey coach at another school back when Brooks had played for Trout Creek High. "You're still interviewing candidates, aren't you?"

"Candidates?"

"For my job."

"It's your job," she assured him. "For as long as you choose to keep it." Apparently she didn't figure that would be very long. "I'll find you some office space and work on that schedule with you."

"Okay then. I'll follow you back to the school, and we'll talk." *Just talk,* he reminded himself as he eased away from her—from the sweet temptation of that full mouth. He forced himself to head toward the Jeep.

"Aren't you forgetting something?" she asked.

He glanced back, surprised. Had she wanted him to kiss her? "What?"

"Your daughter."

Moments later he walked back into the inn and laughter erupted.

"Forget someone?" Buzz asked. The old hockey fanatic was holding the baby in his arms.

Hell. How had he forgotten her? Sure, she'd only been with him a few days. But he worried that his forgetfulness was about more than a change in his routine or even the concussion. He'd inherited a certain gene from his mother—the out-of-sight, out-of-mind one.

Except that he struggled to forget about Priscilla Andrews even when she was out of sight.

"It's lack of sleep, son," his dad said gently, as if trying to reassure him. "We'll get you some help. You've been the one staying up late with her. Me and the boys will pitch in more."

He shook his head. "They've got school. You've got work. And she's *my* responsibility."

He wouldn't give up as easily as his mother had; he'd stick it out as long as he could—despite that pressure on his chest, pushing the breath from his lungs so that he had to struggle for air.

Chapter Eight

Priscilla leaned back in her desk chair and drew in a breath so thick with the scent of fried potatoes she could nearly taste the salt and grease. "Tater Tots day in the cafeteria?" she asked her sister, the lunch lady.

In her white—or mostly white, given the food stains—uniform, Maureen grinned. "Do you want me to bring you some? I could reheat 'em."

Priscilla's empty stomach roiled at the thought of mushy tots. "No thanks."

"Have you had any lunch yet?" Due to their age difference, Maureen often acted more like Priscilla's mother than her sister.

"No, Mom," she mocked her sibling. "I had a meeting with Principal Drover. There was no time to grab anything."

Maureen gave an unladylike snort that would have had their mother puckering her face in disapproval. "I'm sure he ate something."

Priscilla shook her head. "No. He was going to eat at home with his wife, since he was leaving early."

"As usual. And left you with all the work—as usual."

"I don't mind," Priscilla assured her. It wasn't as though she had anything else to do. Trout Creek didn't offer a lot in the way of entertainment. Or single men. "This is what I want," she reminded her sister as well as herself. "If I've already been doing the job. The school board will have to give it to me when he finally retires."

"*If* he ever retires," Maureen said. "And if you keep doing his job for him, he won't need to."

Priscilla shrugged. "That's fine, too. At least I'm doing the job I love."

"You love it? Really?" Maureen arched a brow.

She laughed at the doubt on her sister's face. "Yes, I do. This is what I studied so hard for."

"To spend 24/7 in school?" Maureen shook her head pityingly.

"I enjoy my job," she insisted. And she was good at it. Since she'd been hired, a higher percentage of Trout Creek graduates had enrolled in college.

"You need more than this job," her sister said. "You need a man in your life."

Brooks immediately sprang to mind. But she pushed him away, as she had every other time she'd thought of him over the past few weeks. They'd finally worked out that schedule, setting up a tryout date and subsequent practices. Until the hockey games started, she really didn't need to see much more of him. Except every time she closed her eyes, she pictured his grinning face, those dark eyes full of laughter and passion and the trace of fear he couldn't hide behind cocky bravado.

He was scared and overwhelmed. And she didn't blame him. But she couldn't help him.

She had, however, showed up at the Icehouse to supervise tryouts and practices. It was part of her duties as athletic director to make sure he could handle his job and the kids. But she'd stayed in the stands and just watched, telling herself that she didn't need to talk to him. She didn't *want* to talk to him, to have him stand so close and peer so intently into her eyes that she thought he was going to kiss her again. That she hoped he would...

"Did you hear me?" Maureen asked. "You need to start seeing someone."

"Okay, Mom," she teased again. Their mother constantly nagged Priscilla to find another husband.

Maureen laughed, a little uneasily though. "Stan keeps telling me that I'm turning into my mother." She shuddered. "Say it ain't so."

"Um...you know I can't tell a lie."

"I know. You were always the perfect one."

Priscilla snorted now. "I'm a far cry from perfect."

"Maybe," Maureen replied skeptically. "But it doesn't stop you from trying."

That was true. She had tried to be the perfect wife, the perfect mother, but she'd failed miserably at both. At least she had her career. Here she succeeded every time a kid graduated and went on to college or the military or a good job.

"So, nag, did you come visit me just to make sure I've eaten?"

Maureen smiled. "No. I envy your appetite and your figure, especially since someone talked me into chaperoning the homecoming dance this weekend and I need to find a new dress." She patted her full hips. "*Someone* has to make the sacrifice to ensure all that food is safe for the kids to eat."

"You're such a martyr," Priscilla teased.

"Yup, that's me. A fat Joan of Arc. So since you got me this job and talked me into chaperoning, you're going to have to go dress shopping with me."

"Sure," she agreed, warming to the thought of a trip to the mall in the city.

"And you need a new dress, too," Maureen said.

"Why?" She shrugged. "I have my usual standby."

Her sister looked disgusted. "That black sack you wear to funerals?"

"It's timeless and classy."

"It's boring and ugly."

"So?" She didn't choose her clothes to draw attention to her body. Growing up the proverbial "ugly duckling," she'd learned to use her brains and determination to get ahead—not her looks.

"You need to dress up more."

"Why?" she asked again.

"Because there'll finally be a single man who's under forty and over eighteen at the dance this year."

Confusion furrowed Priscilla's brow. "Who?"

"Brooks."

She laughed. "He's not going to be there."

"Why not?" Maureen asked, her eyes wide with surprise. "Don't you need more chaperones? Isn't that why you roped me into helping?"

She had roped Maureen into helping because she

figured her sister needed a night away from her younger kids and husband. "I really only want school employees to act as chaperones for the homecoming dance."

"He is a school employee now," Maureen reminded her.

"If I'd had my choice, he wouldn't be." She'd interviewed some better candidates, retired teachers who would have loved the part-time position of hockey coach.

"You really turned down Brooks Hoover?"

She almost choked, then swallowed hard. "For a job."

"Yeah." Her sister's eyes widened with curiosity. "What else would you have turned him down for?"

Even now, weeks later, her lips tingled at the memory of that kiss. "Uh…babysitting…"

Maureen reached across the desk and grabbed her hand. "He asked you to babysit?"

"Yeah…"

Her sister squeezed her fingers. "You should tell him about…"

"About what?" Priscilla asked. "Ancient history? It doesn't matter anymore."

"It'll always matter," Maureen said, her voice sympathetic. "What you have to remember is that it wasn't your fault. It was a tragedy you couldn't have prevented."

That was not what her husband had thought. Even though he'd tried to hide it, Priscilla had seen the accusation in his eyes. He'd blamed her for bringing home germs from the school where she'd worked. But none of the kids had had meningitis.

Tears stung Priscilla's eyes, but she blinked them back. "It's fine, really. I actually did watch her once."

"You did?"

She gave a sharp nod. "She's a beautiful baby."

"With his genes?" Maureen let out a lusty chuckle. "Of course she's beautiful. You really should ask him to chaperone."

The only problem with Brooks being a chaperone was who would chaperone *him?*

WITH A JERK, Brooks awoke—Faith clutched tight against his chest. She cried out, then settled back against him. How had he fallen asleep? Probably because she had kept him awake all night.

The real question was what had jarred him from his sleep. His skin tingled, as if someone was staring at him. He glanced toward the open door of the small office next to the gym that Priscilla had assigned to him. If he remembered correctly, it had once been the janitor's closet. A woman leaned against the jamb. Even in the shadow of the dark gymnasium, her body was all lean lines and full curves.

"Priscilla?" he asked, then cleared the rasp from his throat. He glanced at his watch. How long had he been asleep? To figure that out, he'd have to know when he'd nodded off.

"It's me," she confirmed as she stepped inside his office, dragging her heels across the worn linoleum as though reluctant to get any closer to him.

"I expected you to be at every practice to make sure I'm not corrupting the kids." He chuckled. "But now you're even spying on me here?"

"I'm not spying on you."

"You were just standing there, not saying anything," he reminded her. And exactly how long had she been in the doorway?

"I didn't want to wake you," she explained. "You look like you could use the sleep."

He pushed a hand through his tousled hair. "That's no lie. But why don't you speak to me when you stop by at practice?"

"I don't want to interrupt—you're busy with the kids."

He suspected she was busy, too—busy avoiding him. He should have been relieved that she hadn't found a reason to fire him. But every time he caught a glimpse of her in the Icehouse, his pulse quickened with excitement. Then she would walk out without saying a word and that excitement would turn to disappointment.

"You don't have practice tonight?" she asked.

"Had to give 'em a night off," he said.

"And yourself, too."

He swallowed his frustration. She was still determined to think the worst of him. He wouldn't disappoint her by explaining that he'd wanted the kids to take a break because their muscles were already strained. To force them to practice again would have risked serious injuries. "Yeah…"

"So why are you here?" She stepped closer, her gaze on the baby, who slept against his shoulder. "With her?"

"Faith," he said.

"Faith?" Her green eyes widened in surprise. "How do you know her name? Did you find her mother?"

"No." The sheriff's inquiries hadn't turned up any new information. To help the investigation, Brooks had offered to call some of his teammates, but his dad had shot down the idea concerned the press would get hold of the story. Rex worried that other women, not her mother, might try to claim the baby. Brooks just had to trust that Faith's real mom would come back on her own. But Brooks had lost his trust in women a long time ago.

"So you named her?"

"She needed a name." He rubbed his finger across the baby's cheek. "And it seems to fit." He'd been digging deep within himself, looking for faith that he could handle all his new responsibilities.

"Faith…"

The baby opened an eye and glanced around. "I—I don't think she's going to grow up hating you over that name." Priscilla sounded wistful.

"I'm sure she'll find another reason." He was also certain that in time he would give her one. "And that might not stay her name."

"Why not? You think you'll change your mind?"

He shook his head. "No, but her mother could have given her a different name." But if she had, why wouldn't she have written it in her brief note?

"Faith's a good name," Priscilla said. "Now, you never answered my question—what are you doing here?"

He gestured at the pad on his desk. "I'm still trying to figure out my team."

She leaned over the desk and tilted her head to read his writing. He sucked in a breath as the neckline of her gray sweater dipped to reveal the curve of her breasts. He tensed.

Priscilla tapped his pad, drawing his attention from

her cleavage back to the scribbles he'd made on the paper. "You don't have many names written down. A lot more kids showed up to the official tryout."

"If I put half those kids in a game, they'd get killed out there. I'll let 'em practice, but I can't play 'em." He knew how quickly someone could get seriously hurt, even if prepared.

"You're used to playing with professionals. These are just kids."

"All those pros start out as kids with a hell of a lot of talent."

"Not every high school player has the talent to go pro. You know the odds are against anyone from a high school team becoming a pro athlete in any sport. That's why I insist that the emphasis at Trout Creek be on academics now. They need to be fully prepared for the reality of their futures."

Maybe he would have been, had she been the assistant principal back when he was in school. But would anyone have gotten through to Brooks? All he'd ever wanted to do was play. Still did.

He sighed. "You're right. But I made it pro." And he would make it back to the pro league again. "There are a couple of kids out there who might, too."

"Your brothers?"

He nodded. "Brad's got incredible speed and puck control. And his brains make up for what he lacks in muscle. And Ryan." He shook his head. "He's strong and fearless. I don't think there's anything he can't handle. But I can't play both of them the entire game." Despite the shorter periods in high school hockey, he couldn't risk his brothers' futures by having them on the ice so often they got hurt. "Your nephew's good, too. He's one of the faster skaters. He needs to be out there with Brad, not in the net. But he's the only one with goalie experience. Except for Debbie."

"Just so you know, I never suspended Debbie from the game. She chose not to finish out the season last spring. And I talked to her recently," Priscilla confided. "She doesn't want to play."

In the corner of the tiny office, static buzzed from the old black-and-white television. "These are some tapes from last season," he said. "They weren't great." Which was probably why he'd fallen asleep watching them. "But she was. And she loved the game."

Priscilla heard the love in his own voice—but it was for a sport, not a person. He gestured toward the screen, and she watched the goalie and her big defenseman throw their arms around each other after a save. When she saw how tightly and how long Debbie hung on to Ryan, she realized it wasn't Debbie's love of the game she was watching. It was her love for Brooks's brother.

Since the younger Hoover boys tried to emulate their older brother, they dated cheerleaders and perky, popular girls. Ryan dating Debbie would have been like Brooks dating Priscilla back in high school—something that never would have happened then. Or probably even now.

"She might still love the game," she said, "but she doesn't want to play with the team anymore."

"Why not? The guys didn't hassle her. They really respect her and want her back."

She gestured toward the frozen frame—showing

Debbie's arms wound tight around Ryan. "I don't think she wants their *respect*. At least not his."

Brooks stared at the couple. "If you're right…" He shook his head. "Poor girl." Obviously he knew his brother well, despite having spent so much time away.

Priscilla sighed in commiseration. "She's coming to school regularly again, and her grades are better than they were before. But I don't think you're going to talk her into playing."

Brooks nodded. "She didn't even come to tryouts. But if I can't get her, I really need Erik Brouwer back. He tried out, but said you haven't lifted his academic suspension from last year."

"Erik's grades have improved. If he wants to come back, I'll allow it. On one condition…" Priscilla bit her lip, surprised that she was going to do this.

He arched his brows above dark eyes that sparkled with mischief. "Really? What's your condition?"

"I need you to chaperone the homecoming dance next weekend."

He leaned back in his chair, the smile sliding from his handsome face. "Really?"

"Yes."

"But I thought you didn't trust me with the kids."

She nodded. "I didn't, but you did get them to clean the toilet paper off my trees. They listen to you. I just have to trust that you'll say the right things to them."

"And do you trust me?" he asked, his gaze intent on her face, as if her reply really mattered to him.

"No," she honestly admitted. "But I'll be there to make sure you stay in line."

That cocky grin lifted his mouth again. "So you'll be chaperoning my chaperoning?"

"Yes."

"It'll be loud?" he asked with a wince. "And the kids will be out of control?"

"Yes. I haven't been at a homecoming dance yet where I haven't had to throw someone out. That'll be your job, by the way. And I always have to suspend someone afterward for the trouble they caused."

He flinched, as if remembering his own experiences.

"Will you do it?" she asked. "You'll have to wear a suit and tie," she warned him.

"As a chaperone?"

"We all dress up."

"So you'll dress up, too?" he asked. That spark of mischief was back in his dark eyes.

"I'll wear a dress," she said. No matter what her sister tried to get her to buy at the mall, she planned to wear her "black sack."

"You'll give me Erik back?"

"Yes."

"Then I'll do it."

She chuckled at the expression of dread on his handsome face. "To make this sacrifice to get a player back, you must really love the game."

"Hockey's been my life for most of my life."

"Is coaching enough?"

"Until I can play again, it has to be."

And now she had her confirmation that the minute he was reinstated, he would be back on the ice and far away from Trout Creek. After seeing him with the baby and with his brothers, she'd thought she might have misjudged him—that maybe he'd be able to stay in his hometown now that he was older and could appreciate the love and support it offered. But then, he hadn't come home for the same reasons she had.

Chapter Nine

Sweat dampened Brooks's palms as he waited in Coach
Cook's living room. He hadn't been called to the house,
the way he had all those times when he'd been on the
Trout Creek High hockey team. This time he had asked
to see the coach, but nerves tightened the muscles in
Brooks's stomach, anyway.

A clunk and rattle of metal drew his attention to the
arched doorway. His jaw dropped at the sight of Coach
Cook shuffling across the hardwood floor behind a
walker. His daughter, Sonya, held his elbow, steering
and supporting him more than the walker.

"B-B-Brooks," Coach stammered, his speech slurred
from the stroke that had changed the man from the
intimidating giant Brooks remembered into a frail skele-
ton.

After a brief hesitation, he covered his shock and
stepped forward. "It's great to see you, Coach."

Half the older man's mouth lifted. "N-n-no, it's not."

"Well, not like this," Brooks admitted. "I was sorry
to hear about your health."

"W-wish I had my health," he said.

The coach's daughter helped him into a well-worn leather recliner and then smiled at Brooks. Lines of fatigue creased her face, and circles darkened her eyes, making her look much older than her forty-some years. "He appreciated that you sent the card and the DVDs."

"E-everybody else sent d-damn flowers," the coach said.

Brooks laughed. "Yeah, I didn't figure you for the flower type, Coach."

"O-or fruit. I can barely move my mouth and p-people've b-been s-sending me a-apples…."

And Brooks had worried that sending hockey DVDs had been insensitive. "So how are you doing now?" he asked.

"He's doing much better," his daughter replied with another smile, this one forced.

"N-not good enough," the coach protested. "H-had that damn stroke…"

"It's just been a few months," Brooks reminded him. "You gotta give it time. Give yourself some time." He had to remind himself of that, as well—to give fatherhood and coaching time. He couldn't expect to handle something he'd never done—and had never expected to do—easily.

"S-seven months ago," Coach corrected. "Had to have the damn wr-wrestling coach finish out last season for me. B-but you didn't come here to talk about my health, Brooks."

"I intended to come by to visit," he insisted, "but I got busy." Busier than he had thought he could ever be in Trout Creek.

"Took my job," the old man complained, but his faded blue eyes twinkled. "You're coach now."

Brooks shook his head. "I haven't earned that title yet."

"Y-you will...."

"I'm not sure how to coach like you did."

"Y-you can't," his former hero informed him. "You can only coach your own way. Th-that's how you'll reach the kids."

"These kids can be reached?" he asked with a chuckle. "Maybe with a stick upside the head."

The coach's mouth twisted into that half smile again. "R-Ryan does remind m-me of you."

"To my father's great disappointment," Brooks said.

Coach shook his head. "Sheriff Hoover is v-very proud of you."

Maybe as an athlete, but Brooks had yet to prove himself as a man. That was why he still insisted on caring for Faith himself as much as he could. The town tried to help, the way Brooks knew they had with Coach. But a man had his pride, had things he needed to do on his own. "I'm trying to figure out this whole coaching thing," he admitted. "But I need help."

"I—I can't...take the cold anymore. Can't walk around a rink..."

"I'd love your help," Brooks admitted. "But I know that's not possible for a couple more weeks." He winked when the old man grinned at his faith in him. "While I wait for you to get better, I could use Debbie's help."

"Debbie?" the girl's mother asked. "But she quit the team."

"Do you know why?" he pressed.

The old man thumped his chest. "I—I'm the reason...."

"You made her quit?" Brooks asked. That surprised him less than the fact he'd let a girl play.

Coach Cook shook his head, his mouth moving as if he wanted to speak but couldn't manage the words. So his daughter spoke for him. "He thinks Debbie quit so she could help me take care of him."

The fiercely independent man that Brooks remembered would have hated that. "Do you think she's ready to play again?"

While the coach nodded as vigorously as his weak muscles allowed, Debbie's mother hesitated. Maybe she needed her daughter's help and wouldn't appreciate Brooks's interference.

A door opened, and a female voice called out, "Who's here?"

"Brooks Hoover," Sonya called back.

Debbie hurried into the living room, her cheeks flushed from the cold. "Hey, Mr. Hoover. Did you bring the baby with you?"

He shook his head. "No. Miss Andrews is watching Faith for me." He could have asked someone else. Myrtle had promised to be available whenever he needed her. Even his dad would have taken her. But there was something about the expression on Priscilla's face when she looked at the baby, that mixture of pain and longing and wistfulness, that told Brooks Priscilla *needed* to watch her.

"Faith?" the girl asked. "That's her name?"

"Yes."

"It's pretty." She blinked. "And Miss Andrews has her?"

"Yes. She agreed to look after her while I came over to talk to you." Albeit she had agreed almost as reluctantly as she had the other time he'd asked her to take care of the baby. But he'd pointed out that bringing an infant around the coach might be too much for the old man, especially if she started crying or fussing. Brooks had also lied and told her no one else was available.

"Miss Andrews is great," Debbie said. "She's so nice. And smart and pretty."

Brooks's heart slammed against his ribs as he realized the truth of the girl's words—and the fact she must have assumed Priscilla was babysitting because they were seeing each other. He swallowed hard and agreed, "Yeah, she's great."

He couldn't remember if he'd ever met anyone like Priscilla, someone who cared so much about everyone else. Every student at Trout Creek High mattered to her; she felt responsible for each of them, from trying to secure their academic future to ensuring their health with her free flu shot program. He winced, remembering that she had even persuaded teachers and coaches to participate. Despite all the stitches he'd had over the years, or maybe because of them, he hated needles. But she'd talked him into it with the argument that he didn't want to bring germs home to Faith, and she'd stood by as Nurse Trudy administered the injection in the office where he'd spent too much time growing up.

He shook off thoughts of the beautiful assistant principal and focused on the teenager. "You're great, too, Debbie," he praised her. "I've watched footage of last season."

"We sucked," she murmured, then reddened as she glanced at her grandfather.

The old man smiled that lopsided smile and nodded. "Hard to make a team with only a few good players."

"You were one of them," Brooks told her.

She lifted her broad shoulders in a shrug.

"If you came back, I think we might have a chance of winning. Brad's playing now." He was proud that his youngest brother had made the varsity team his freshman year. "He's really good. And Ryan—"

She shook her head. "No. I can't."

Damn, Priscilla was probably right about the girl's crush on Ryan. "Can't or don't want to?"

"Can't," she insisted. "Miss Andrews pointed out that my grades are more important, especially now. This is my junior year. Colleges will be looking at these marks when I apply."

The only thing colleges had cared about with Brooks was how he'd played.

"I'm sorry, Mr. Hoover, I have to think about my future."

She wasn't the only one....

HORRIFIED BY WHAT SHE SAW, Priscilla could only stare, eyes wide with shock, stomach knotted with dread. A cry burned in her throat, but she couldn't utter it or she might awaken the sleeping baby nestled in her arms.

Although the quality of the video was gritty, Brooks's image was clear. First his helmet flew off, skittering across the rink. Then he fell back, and his head slammed onto the ice.

Her breath caught, a gasp slipping through her lips. He lay there, not moving. The camera panned to his face, where blood trailed from his ear, across his cheek, and trickled onto the ice. "Oh my God," she whispered. He'd cracked his skull.

"Sports Central obtained footage of this practice from five weeks ago, of a fight between Brooks Hoover and a teammate resulting in an injury that has sidelined Hoover for the season," the commentator reported. "According to a source at River City Memorial Hospital, Hoover was in a coma for days and may have sustained permanent brain damage from his fractured skull."

Her hand shaking, she grabbed up the remote and paused the digital recorder on the image of Brooks lying there lifelessly. Even when she'd caught him sleeping in his office, he hadn't been completely still. There'd been a tension to his body, in the line of his square jaw, in the flash of the dimple in his cheek.

There was no tension, no spark, no trace of his energy and indomitable spirit in that body lying on the ice. The image blurred as tears welled in her eyes. The press might have been sensationalizing the story some, but she didn't doubt he'd had a close call, closer than any other in his reckless life.

As if sensing her emotional state, the baby whimpered and stirred. "Shh, Faith," she murmured softly, lulling the child back to sleep. "It's okay. He's okay."

A knock drew her attention away from the TV, but before she could lift the baby from her lap, the door opened and Brooks stepped inside, shaking raindrops from his damp curls. He flashed that grin, the one that had the dimple piercing his cheek and mischief dancing in his eyes.

Her breath hitched, and she tried to curve her lips into a smile in response. But instead of seeing him now, vibrantly alive in front of her, she saw him lying on the ice, the blood pooling beneath his head.

"Everything all right?" he asked, dropping to his knees in front of the couch. He leaned over the baby on her lap and ran his fingertip along the delicate line of the infant's jaw.

She nodded. "Great. She's been sleeping since you dropped her off."

"Sheesh, woman, I need to bring you home with me."

Priscilla's heart rate sped up. "Why—why would you say that?"

He grinned. "Because you're about the only one who can get Faith here to sleep. The boys think she's a werewolf, that as soon as the sun goes down she starts howling at the moon."

"That's probably why she's sleeping now," Priscilla pointed out. "She's all tired out."

He shook his head. "The more tired she is, usually the more fussy she is. But with you, she must feel safe. That's why she sleeps so well over here."

Priscilla couldn't look at him, couldn't let him know how his innocent comment had affected her. Faith shouldn't feel safe with her—of all people.

"It's no wonder if you've been holding her the

whole time," he said. "You didn't have to. I brought her foldout bed."

He had set up the portable crib for her, but Priscilla couldn't bring herself to lay the baby in it. She'd needed to *watch* her—until the special report from Sports Central had broken into the six o'clock news. Only that footage had pulled her attention from Faith.

"I didn't mind holding her," she said, then tensed in surprise at her admission. While she was nervous and hypervigilant, she wasn't as scared as she'd been the last time she'd watched the baby. Faith had been fine then. And she seemed fine now.

Better than Brooks.

"Well, your arms are probably sleeping as soundly as she is," he said, lifting the baby from her. He cuddled her close for a moment, pressing a kiss to her forehead, before he rose and carried her to that portable crib. "She gets heavier the longer you hang on to her."

"I'm fine," Priscilla said.

He turned back to her, studying her face. "You don't look fine. What did I say that upset you?"

She shook her head. "It wasn't what you said." She picked up the remote. The television had gone into standby mode, the logo for the satellite company bouncing across the dark screen. But she clicked the play button and his image reappeared.

"Damn it." He uttered the curse with a ragged sigh. "I didn't know anyone recorded that."

"It looks like cell-phone footage," she said, as if it mattered. Nothing mattered but him. "Are you all right?"

"I was," he murmured, dropping onto the couch next to her. He took the remote from her hand, his own shaking slightly, and rewound to the beginning of the report. More curses slipped through his lips.

"You didn't want anyone to know how badly you were hurt," she said.

He clicked off the TV and tossed down the remote. "I wasn't hurt as badly as they said."

"As I saw?" she asked. "You were bleeding...." Fear rose up to choke her, but she swallowed it down. "You have a head injury. You were in a coma."

"Not as long as they're saying."

"But you were in a coma."

"For a few days."

She nodded. "I remember the sheriff leaving town for a while several weeks ago. Myrtle stayed with the boys."

He grinned. "Yeah, my dad was there. I woke up with a hell of headache, probably because he was yelling at me for being a fool. I mean, going out on the ice without my helmet strap clasped. I'd bench any of my team for doing that."

She nodded in sudden understanding. "I remember hearing you yell at them once about that. You're very safety conscious with them." It was just another thing about which she'd misjudged him.

"Yeah, Coach Hoover's number one rule—do as I say, not as I do." Brooks pushed a hand through his still-damp curls. "Now everyone's going to see what an idiot I was."

"You weren't the one who started that fight," she reminded him. "Your own teammate attacked you."

"He didn't attack me. He just shoved me. If I'd had my helmet on right, I wouldn't have been hurt at all."

And here she thought he was a man who didn't take responsibility. "If he hadn't shoved you, you wouldn't have been hurt."

"Graham's a friend," he said, defending the goalie. "And I actually did start the fight."

"But you'd just skated out on the ice…"

"It was about something I did off the ice."

Realization dawning, she asked, "Or someone? Was that fight over a woman?"

"It was stupid," he said. "I was stupid."

"Was she someone special?" Priscilla murmured.

"To him. I didn't know that, though, or I wouldn't have…"

He didn't have to spell it out for her. "Has any girl ever been special to you?"

His gaze slid over her before he glanced to the baby sleeping in the crib.

Helpless and beautiful, Faith made it impossible for a person not to care about her, even though Priscilla had tried. She couldn't get attached, for so many reasons. Brooks wasn't going to stay in Trout Creek, and he'd take his daughter with him when he left. Or the baby's mother would return to claim her.

Either way, the baby wasn't going to stay in Priscilla's life any more than Brooks was. "She's special," she admitted, but when she turned back to him, he was staring at her.

"I was actually thinking about you."

"Me?" Her voice squeaked.

His dimple flashed, and his eyes brightened despite the dark circles beneath them. "I haven't stopped thinking about you since that kiss."

She hadn't stopped thinking about him since then, either. Just talking about it now had her lips tingling again. Suddenly, she realized how close they were on the couch, his hard thigh pressed against hers. His arm rested across the back, just behind her shoulders—not touching, but so close she could feel the heat of it, just as she did his leg. Her pulse quickened and her blood warmed.

Then her heart stopped beating altogether when he said, "And I haven't stopped wanting you."

Chapter Ten

Priscilla stared at Brooks, her green eyes wide with doubt. "No, you don't." Her breath shuddered out. "You can't want *me*."

The doubt, even more than the vulnerability she betrayed every time she looked at Faith, twisted his stomach. "How can you not believe me?"

The corners of her mouth lifted but didn't quite form a real smile. "You're you."

"That's not why you don't believe me," he said. "It's not because you think I'm a playboy. Or that I'm just trying to get you into bed—"

"You're not?"

He grinned now, sheepishly, and dropped his arm from the couch to her shoulders. "Okay, I'll admit that I'd like to...."

She tensed and shifted away from him, into the corner of the couch. "I know you're bored, being home in Trout Creek, but there are other single women besides me."

"I don't want just any woman," he said. And he stopped, stunned, as he realized he spoke the truth.

She cocked her head, scrutinizing him as if he was some kid trying to sell her a sorry excuse for losing his homework. "Brooks…"

"This isn't about me," he insisted. "It's about you. I've never met anyone like you before."

"You've known me since kindergarten," she reminded him.

And because Trout Creek was so small, they had had many classes together. But he shook his head. "I didn't know you."

"We didn't exactly move in the same social circles," she agreed.

"No, I was a dumb jock who didn't realize how special you are. I've never known anyone who cares so much about everyone else but herself."

Her brow furrowed with confusion. "I don't…."

"Yes, you do. You pitch in wherever you're needed at the school. I've seen you helping out in the cafeteria, answering phones in the office. And when a teenage girl's crying, she heads right to you, knowing you'll give her a shoulder and some sound advice."

"You make me sound like Dear Abby."

"You are," he said. Dear to everyone who really knew her. "Not only are you selfless but you're so damn beautiful…"

She laughed now, but it sounded false. "You really must have lasting brain damage from that fight."

"I have a concussion," he admitted. "That knocked some sense into me."

"I think it knocked you for a loop," she said, her eyes warming with sympathy. "You're scared that you're not going to be able to play anymore, that you're going to be stuck here in Trout Creek."

He sighed. "That may be true, but so is everything I've just said about you."

"You're a charmer, Brooks Hoover. And a heartbreaker." She smiled. "Always were. Probably always will be. I know better than to get involved with you—and especially not to fall in love with you."

He should have been relieved, but something tightened in his chest. It wasn't that he wanted her to care about him. As she'd said, he didn't want to be stuck in Trout Creek.

"That's fine," he assured her and himself. "That's good. Then it won't get messy." He leaned closer, his chest nearly touching her breasts.

She expelled a shaky breath that teased his lips. "What won't get messy? What are you doing?"

"I'm going to show you just how special you are." He closed his arms around her shoulders again, pulling her closer.

But she shoved her hands between them. "I don't want to get involved with you."

"We won't get involved," he said. "We both know we're not right for each other." He was pretty damn sure he wasn't right for anyone. "But we can have some fun. When's the last time you let yourself have fun?"

Her forehead creased, as if she were considering his question. Then she shook her head. "This is a bad idea."

"Probably," he agreed. "You're my boss." He leaned even closer and skimmed his lips across the corner of her mouth. Her breath sighed out across his skin. "But don't worry. I won't sue you for harassment."

"Who's harassing whom?" she pointed out, her hands grabbing his shoulders. But instead of shoving him back, she clutched him closer. "If this is some joke…"

His control snapped, and he swung her up in his arms. After checking to make sure Faith slept peacefully, he carried Priscilla to her bedroom. When he'd picked up his daughter that Saturday four weeks ago, he'd noticed the oval mirror standing in the corner of the small room. He set Priscilla on her feet in front of it now, her back to him.

"What are you doing?" she asked, twisting her neck to stare up at him.

He pressed his thumb under her chin and tilted her face back toward the mirror. "Look at yourself. I don't think you've ever really seen yourself, Priscilla."

"It's my mirror." Her eyes sparkled with amusement. "I've looked in it before."

"But you haven't seen what you really look like," he insisted. "You haven't seen what I see."

"What do you see?" she asked.

"Beauty. True beauty. The kind that goes beneath the surface." Beneath the unflattering clothes. He clenched his fingers in the waistband of her thick gray sweater and pulled it up and over her head.

Goose bumps appeared on her pale skin as she stood between him and the mirror, wearing only her skirt and bra. It was white and no-nonsense—just like her.

His fingers trembled as he fumbled with the clasp of her skirt before it dropped to the floor next to her sweater. Like her bra, her underpants were plain and white.

Heat rushed up, flushing her face and breasts. "You're used to women who shop at Victoria's Secret," she said.

"I don't care about your clothes." He cared about her, and that realization staggered him. But to prove the point about her underwear, he unhooked her bra and pushed down the straps so that it fell away from her breasts. He shuddered slightly with appreciation and desire. "You are so beautiful."

His fingers shaking, he slid her panties over her lean hips until they pooled around her heels. "Damn, woman…"

In the mirror, her gaze met his—her eyes wide with surprise and acceptance. "I *am* beautiful," she murmured, her voice soft with awe as she surveyed her image in the mirror.

He slid his hands over her skin, his so dark against her pale complexion. She shivered, as if chilled, but her flesh was warm to his touch. Hot, even. "You're gorgeous.…" Inside and out. He skimmed his hands over her nipples until they pebbled against his palms.

"We—we can't do this," she said. "Faith is just in the other room."

"She's out," he reminded her. Priscilla gave the baby a sense of security he was afraid he would never be able to offer her.

"Brooks." She turned in his arms.

He grimaced at her tone, worried that she was going to push him away again. But instead, she wound her arms around his neck and pulled his head down to hers. Her lips trailed across his cheek, her breath warm in his ear. "Let me kiss it," she suggested, "and make it all better."

That pressure settled on his chest again, but he didn't feel trapped. He just *felt*. She'd said she wouldn't get involved. But what about him? Would he—*could* he—fall in love?

Her silky lips brushed across his, once, twice, teasing, before she pulled back. "I'm so glad you're all right," she said. "Seeing you on the ice like that *scared* me."

She probably hadn't been half as scared as he was right now. His hands trembled slightly as he lifted them, sliding them over her bare back. He pulled her closer, tight against his chest, his heart pounding fast and hard. "I'm all right," he lied.

"I'm glad," she said, her arms tightening around him. "Because I expect you to show me a good time."

That was all she expected from him. And she was all right with that, Priscilla realized. She had been so serious, so driven for much of her life, and all it had ever brought her was disappointment. Now she didn't want to think about anything—that the infant sleeping in her living room wasn't hers, or that this man was not the one to love her forever.

She wanted to push those thoughts from her mind and just feel—everything that Brooks's touch promised her she would feel. Her hands shaking with adrenaline, she yanked up his shirt and pulled it over his head. Bare skin stretched taut over sculpted muscles. She dipped her head and pressed her lips against his chest.

He groaned and clutched his fingers in her hair, tugging her head up. His mouth covered hers with such passion her lips parted with a moan.

Damn, the man could kiss....

And his hands... He touched her everywhere, his fingertips caressing her skin, raising goose bumps of excitement. His tongue slid between her lips and then over them, stroking and caressing just like his hands. She shivered in anticipation, unable to back out now.

She wouldn't shove him away again. She couldn't. She wanted him so much and wanted what he could make her feel even more. Pleasure...

He carried her to the bed, laying her atop the flowered, flannel sheets. Then he shucked off his jeans and briefs and followed her down, his hard, muscled body covering hers. Like his face, his body bore faint scars. Skin puckered where stitches must had pulled it together. But those marks only added to his sexiness. She ran her fingertips along a ridge on his side and another over his hip. His body had taken so much abuse.

"I love the feel of your hands on me," he murmured, his voice low and rough with desire. "The way you touch me..."

She loved touching him, stroking her fingers across skin stretched taut over finely honed muscle. Since he'd kissed her, she had dreamed of having him like this, naked in her bed. But she hadn't believed it would ever happen.

He kissed her again, so deeply and passionately that she moaned once more. Her body trembled, pressure already building inside her.

His hands moved over her again, over the tips of her breasts and the curve of her hip. His fingers stroked through her curls and then slid inside her. She shuddered and cried out, nipping at the hard muscles of his shoulder.

He groaned. So she touched him intimately, too, wrapping her fingers around the thick length of him. Then she pumped her hand up and down. He pulled away. "Slow down, we can take our time."

He pushed her back and moved over her, slowly, using his mouth to love every inch of her. He kissed her throat, slid his lips along her collarbone and then closed his mouth over the tip of her breast.

Priscilla arched off the mattress, into his mouth. "Please…"

She needed more. She needed everything he could offer her. She needed Brooks.

Foil rustled, then tore. His erection, sheathed, pushed gently inside her. She arched again and shifted, trying to adjust to him. He was so big. So Brooks. While he thrust inside her, he pressed his lips against hers, imitating with his tongue what he was doing to her body.

She met each thrust, in perfect unison with his every movement—as if they had made love many times before. But even though she'd been married, she'd never felt like this. Pleasure wound through her with unbearable pressure, pulling at her nipples, curling her toes until it broke free, shattering her.

Before she could cry out, he covered her mouth with his. Then he thrust once more and stiffened—and groaned against her lips as he came, too.

Priscilla fought back tears as powerful emotion threatened to overwhelm her.

"Are you okay?" he asked, his voice a rough whisper against her ear.

She nodded. "Fine, fine…"

"You're more than fine," he said, "you're amazing." He pressed a kiss to her cheek, then pulled away and walked naked from the room.

Even though he'd just given her more pleasure than she ever remembered feeling, desire wound through her again, quivering low in her stomach. But moments later, water ran in the adjacent bathroom. Was he leaving?

Of course he was leaving. He wasn't the type to spend the night with a woman, not after she'd given him what he wanted. It was her fault that she wanted more.…

A CRY STARTLED PRISCILLA, awakening her from a dream. But she wasn't sleeping. He was, lying naked and beautiful on the tangled sheets beside her. Dark circles beneath his heavily lashed eyes were the only things that detracted from his masculine beauty.

She slipped from beneath Brooks's possessive arm and pulled on the shirt that she'd dragged off him. Brooks Hoover in *her* bed? She had to be dreaming.

The baby cried out again. That was a sound Priscilla had heard only in her nightmares. Until now.

She hurried into the living room. Kicking her short legs and pumping her fists in the air, Faith wailed lustily. Recognizing the cry as one of frustration, not pain or illness, Priscilla expelled a sigh of relief. Then she lifted the tiny wriggling body from the portable crib. As the baby snuggled against her, Priscilla's heart wrenched with emotion. "You haven't been letting your daddy get much sleep, have you?"

"You called me her daddy," Brooks said, his voice gruff.

He stood just behind her, rubbing sleep from his eyes. Even though he looked exhausted, he'd awakened at his daughter's cry.

"You are," Priscilla stated.

"The DNA results aren't back yet," he admitted.

"No?"

He shook his head. "There was some kind of mix-up at the lab. I had to give another blood sample." He shuddered as if remembering the needle.

She smiled, remembering how the big strong hockey player had blanched when Trudy had administered his flu shot.

"I can't believe it's taking so long," she said, more for something to say than because she doubted him. And to distract herself from the jeans he'd tugged on, which rode tantalizingly low on his lean hips.

"You know what I can't believe," he said, stepping closer to her and wrapping his arms around her waist beneath the now-sleeping Faith. "That you're still single. There must be no eligible men in Trout Creek."

"Except you," she reminded him, then chuckled as his body tensed. "Just kidding. I know you're not the marrying kind." Had Faith's mother gotten pregnant to try to trap him into marriage? But then why not tell him about it? Why just leave her precious baby on his doorstep?

His lips skimmed over the skin exposed by the

gaping neckline of his big shirt. "I'm serious. I don't understand how you're still single."

She drew in a breath, then confessed, "I wasn't always. I'm divorced."

His arm tightened around her waist, pulling her back against his chest. "He's the one, huh?"

She tilted her head to look back at him and see what he was talking about. "The one what?"

"Your ex," he replied, as if that explained everything.

"What about my ex?" Not that she really wanted to discuss Owen or anything else about their brief marriage.

"*He's* the one," Brooks repeated, his voice deep with disgust, "who made you feel less than you are."

She shook her head. "I don't have a clue what you're talking about."

"You have no idea how special you are," he reminded her. "How smart, how beautiful…"

He'd made her see it—standing her in front of that mirror, his hands pulling off her clothes, then gliding over her naked body. She'd never been so turned on or so awed. And although they'd made love, she'd realized that he was right. Brooks Hoover couldn't love her like she deserved to be loved, like her husband should have loved her.

She smiled, though, touched by his compliments. "Brooks, you already got me into bed." If not for the baby in her arms, she would have led him back there. "You don't have to keep charming me."

"Priscilla, what we did…"

"Wasn't serious," she assured him. "I know. We were just having fun." And she couldn't remember the last time she'd forgotten her guilt and her pain and her responsibilities the way she had in his arms.

"Was it fun?" he asked.

"It was…" *Amazing*. Beyond anything she could have imagined. But she didn't want to worry him that she was falling for him. "Fun."

"I can be more than fun," he said, as if she'd offended him.

"Brooks…"

"I can be your friend," he offered.

Even though she'd kept her thoughts to herself, he must have picked up on how much making love with him had meant to her. So now he was going to give her the just-friends speech?

"You look like you could use a friend," he continued. "He really hurt you, didn't he?" He reached around her and ran his fingertip over his sleeping daughter's cheek.

"Who?" she asked, distracted by his display of tenderness. Here was a man who'd started many a fight on the ice, but he couldn't have been more gentle with the baby or with her.

"Your ex," he said. "I'm not the only one who came home to Trout Creek to heal."

How could she have considered a man as perceptive as Brooks Hoover to be a dumb jock? She'd been back for five years, but no one besides her sister had noticed her pain.

She tilted her head again to look up at his handsome face, which was soft with affection as he stared down at Faith. Then his gaze met Priscilla's—and the tenderness was still there.

"Let me be your friend," he persisted. "Tell me what happened, why you're still hurting."

Faith's tiny body tensed, and she opened her mouth and emitted a high-pitched wail. For once the baby's crying didn't send Priscilla into a panic. Brooks took the little girl from her arms. His biceps rippling, he rocked his daughter back and forth.

Priscilla was panicking, but not over the baby. She was afraid that she wanted more from Brooks Hoover than friendship.

Chapter Eleven

Priscilla stood at his side, but Brooks felt as if he'd lost her. She had closed herself off from him, treating him like a stranger despite the fact that he'd just touched and tasted every sexy inch of her.

"Tell me about your marriage," he implored her, wondering what kind of guy would be lucky enough to marry her and then stupid enough to let her go. She was so generous, so loving, so smart....

So tense. She shrugged stiff shoulders. "There's nothing to talk about. In fact, hardly anyone knows I was ever married. It didn't last very long."

"Why not?" he asked.

She didn't meet his gaze. Instead, her attention was focused on the baby.

"Was it over kids?" he asked. She had probably wanted a dozen.

She shook her head. "I don't want to talk about it. It was a long time ago."

"But you're still hurting over it." He could almost

feel her pain, like that dull throb left over from the concussion. "Talk to me about it."

She turned on him now, anger chasing the vulnerability from her deep green eyes. "Why? Are you so bored being back in Trout Creek that even I seem interesting to you?"

Her defensiveness almost made him step back from her. "I am interested in you, Priscilla. I want to know more about you, about your life." He wanted to know everything.

But before he could convince her to confide in him, she glanced at the window. "Someone's coming."

Even though it wasn't late, not even nine according to the clock on her mantel, it was pitch-black outside. Headlights glowed through the darkness as a car headed down the gravel driveway toward her cabin. Brooks recognized the rumble of the powerful engine. "Dad better not have let Ryan drive the Mustang."

Priscilla's eyes widened in horror as she glanced from his bare chest to the shirt she wore. She ran into her bedroom, opening the door a moment later to toss his shirt out. He turned to catch a glimpse of her delectable naked body, but she'd closed the door too fast.

And he wasn't quick enough to pull on his shirt before someone pounded at the door. Through the sheer curtain, Brooks recognized his father's burly build. With a jerk of his head he gestured for his dad to open the door.

"What are you doing here?" he asked, irritated that the old man had interrupted his conversation with Priscilla. When would his dad realize that Brooks wasn't a kid anymore?

"Tracking you down," he replied, his voice sharp. "Don't you answer your damn phone?"

Brooks flinched. "I left it in the Jeep." He hadn't thought he'd be in Priscilla's house long. Had figured he'd just pick up Faith and go. "Are the boys okay?"

His dad nodded. "Yeah. But you got company back at the house."

"Faith's mother?" he asked with a surge of relief and dread. While he wanted his daughter to have a mom, he didn't want to lose the baby. "I was sure she'd come back."

Rex shook his head. "Hopefully she won't come around now. There's a whole damn pack of reporters outside the house."

Brooks cursed. "Thanks for the warning."

"I came for more than the warning," his dad continued. "I'm going to take the baby over to Myrtle's house. Those damn vultures don't need to learn about her."

Brooks chuckled at his dad's naiveté. "If they've been in Trout Creek five minutes, I'm sure they know all about the baby left on my doorstep."

Rex shook his head. "You never did appreciate this town, son. We protect our own. Nobody's going to tell anybody about Faith."

Brooks glanced down at the baby's perfect little face. She was awake and staring up at him with those big, serious eyes of hers. "Maybe they should. Maybe it'll bring her mother back."

His dad laughed now, as if Brooks was the naive one. "And how many other women will claim to be her mother just to get their hooks into you?" He glanced at

Brooks's bare chest and raised a bushy brow. "Or has someone already done that?"

Brooks shook his head. It wasn't any of his father's business what he and Priscilla had done. "Faith threw up on my shirt again," he lied.

Too smart to fall for the story, Rex picked up the shirt Priscilla had tossed out the bedroom door. "Well, you better get dressed and get home. Let 'em see you're alive and well, and maybe they'll leave us the hell alone."

When he'd first gone pro, Brooks had loved the attention of the media, but it had gotten old fast. The best part of playing for the city league had been that most of the sportscasters had lost interest in him. Like Wes's dad, they'd written him off as a has-been. But all it took was a little scandal to provoke a media frenzy. The little scandal wriggled in his arms. Even more than the cell-phone footage of the fight, the press would have a field day when they found out he didn't know the identity of his baby's mother.

"Let me help you get Faith ready to go to Myrtle's," he said. Adept now at snaps and tabs, he quickly changed the baby and fastened her into her car seat. "She's probably hungry," he warned. Having been trapped in a car with her when she wanted a bottle, he didn't envy his father right now.

"Those reporters are hungry, too," Rex reminded him as he headed for the door with the carrier and diaper bag.

Brooks followed and opened the door for him. But his father paused at the threshold, his eyes dark with concern. "Faith isn't the only gal you have to worry about protecting, you know."

It was his father's tone more than the cool night breeze that chilled Brooks. The old man knew that Priscilla had come home to Trout Creek just as wounded as his son had. Maybe more, because Brooks's wounds were only physical.

"I'll be careful," he promised.

His dad walked out with a grin and a parting shot. "I guess that concussion did knock some sense into you. That's the first time you've ever told me that."

Probably because Brooks had known better than to make promises he couldn't keep. He closed the door behind the old man and called to Priscilla, "You can come out now."

PRISCILLA PRESSED her hands to her hot face. She had dressed in jeans and a heavy sweatshirt, but still felt naked and exposed. Through the thin walls in the tiny cabin, she'd overheard their conversation. What if the reporters had followed the sheriff to her house? What if everyone in Trout Creek—in the country—learned that she was notorious playboy Brooks Hoover's latest conquest?

She could kiss her chance of taking over as principal goodbye. Even knowing that, she wanted to kiss Brooks goodbye; she wanted to feel his lips on hers one last time.

A fist knocked at her bedroom door before it creaked open. "Priscilla? Are you all right?"

She nodded. "Of course. But you'd better go." Before the reporters tracked him down at her house.

Frustration etched deep furrows in his forehead. "I'd rather stay here. With you."

"You have to leave," she reminded him, glad now that his dad had interrupted them. Brooks wanted to talk about her past, about her marriage, about her ex, and she had no doubt he would extract every painful detail from her. He'd already intuited more about her than any man—anyone—had since her divorce. She couldn't allow him to get closer, not when she knew for certain she would lose him.

He pushed open the door all the way and stepped into her bedroom. "I don't want to leave before we have a chance to talk."

She smiled. "You'd just rather talk to me than reporters."

He crossed the room to join her at the window, reaching out to run his fingertips along her jaw. "I wouldn't talk. I'd listen."

Her breath caught with surprise and pleasure at both his offer and his seductive touch.

"I think you listen to everyone else, but no one ever listens to you," he said, proving to her once again that he was more than a sexy body. He was smart and perceptive, and she felt vulnerable with him staring into her eyes.

"Maybe I have nothing to say," she pointed out, her breath coming shallow and fast.

He grinned. "You have plenty to say. You just don't want to."

"I have one thing to say." It was the only thing she *could* say without giving him any more of herself. "We had fun. That's all it was. All that it can be."

ALL THAT IT CAN BE.

She was right. He knew she was, but still it rankled. Usually he was the one who said those words, who posted the boundaries of a relationship.

Until now. Until Priscilla Andrews.

Everyone else expected too much of him, especially his dad. And now his brothers. He stared at their faces on the television screen.

"My brother's great," Brad told the sportscaster who held a mike to him. "He could play, but he came back to coach our hockey team to its first division win since he played for Trout Creek High himself."

Behind Brad, Ryan pumped his fist in the air. "Yeah!"

No, Brooks inwardly groaned. Under his inept leadership, the team would be lucky to win one game, let alone the tier or division finals.

"Our regular coach, his old high school coach, had a stroke, so Brooks agreed to take over." Brad continued the spin. Maybe instead of an athlete, the kid should become a politician or a sports agent.

Brooks snorted. But he hadn't when the camera panned to him earlier. On the television screen now, he merely smiled and acknowledged, "I'm lucky to be able to coach them."

Especially since his new boss hadn't wanted him for the job. She'd been right that he wasn't qualified for the position. Except for playing hockey, he wasn't qualified for much of anything.

"How serious was your brain injury?" a reporter asked.

He winked at the camera. "Not serious enough to

justify you all coming up to Trout Creek. I'm fine. Really. I'll be playing next season, and the coach will love me, since I'll have a new appreciation for how hard his job is."

More questions followed as the reporters tried to work up a scandal. But when he downplayed the fight as an accident, they lost interest. Sick of seeing his own face on TV, Brooks clicked the off button on the remote.

Brad had wedged himself between Brooks and Ryan on the family room couch. "So how bad were you hurt? Dad wouldn't let us go with him to see you."

"Yeah, he had Myrtle babysitting us like she's watching your kid tonight," Ryan grumbled.

But Myrtle wasn't babysitting alone tonight; his dad was still over there, leaving Brooks to figure out how much his brothers should know. "I was in a coma, just not as long as they claim."

"Do you have brain damage?" Brad asked.

He shook his head. "No. Just a concussion."

"So, Ryan, you're the only Hoover with brain damage," Brad teased.

Ryan wrapped his beefy arm around his younger brother's neck. "You're going to have brain damage when I'm done with you."

Brad wriggled around, bumping into Brooks as he tried to free himself. "Then who'll do your homework?"

Ryan immediately loosened his grasp when Brooks groaned. Both brothers stared at him.

"You okay?" Brad asked.

"No, I'm worried. You guys are cheating?"

"I wouldn't call it cheating." Brad, the future politician, assumed the spokesperson role again.

"Ms. Andrews will and she'll suspend you both for it—from the school and the team."

Brad's dark eyes widened. "She won't! Dad'll talk to Principal Drover."

Brooks shook his head. "No. Dad needs to stop cleaning up after us and protecting us." He pushed a hand through his hair. "I was hurt bad," he admitted. "There's some concern that another head injury could cause permanent brain damage."

Brad gasped, and his dark eyes welled with tears.

"You won't be able to play anymore?" Ryan asked.

Dread tied knots in Brooks's stomach. He couldn't imagine not playing. "I have to go back to a neurologist and the team doctor to get cleared before I can get reinstated. But I'm sure they were just overreacting in the hospital." After three days in a coma, he'd been pretty out of it when he'd awakened—too out of it to remember everything he'd been told about his medical condition. "I'm sure I'll play again."

It was his whole life. All he had ever wanted. Now he wasn't sure what he wanted—besides more time alone with Priscilla.

"But you can't play," Brad said, his voice cracking with emotion. "You shouldn't risk becoming a vegetable."

Brooks was moved by the boys' reactions to his close scrape. For most of their lives he'd been gone, more stranger than brother to them, but still they cared about him. And he cared about them more than he'd realized— too much to let them make the mistakes he had.

"Hockey is all I know," he admitted. "But I still don't know enough to be a coach. I shouldn't have this job. And if I can't play again, I'm not qualified for any job."

"But you can still be our coach," Brad insisted.

Brooks shook his head. "If Coach Cook wants his job back, it's his."

"Talk about veg—"

"Ryan!" Brooks stopped his brother from finishing the rude remark.

"But he's old," Brad pointed out. "He's going to want to retire. You can stay as coach."

Brooks shook his head. "Not if the team sucks this year."

"But Miss Priss can't fire you because we suck."

"Stop calling her that," he said, automatically defending her. As he'd learned just a couple of hours ago, there was nothing prissy about Priscilla. "And she won't have to," he added. "If I can't turn you guys into a halfway decent team, I'll quit. It wouldn't be fair to you and the other kids if I blow your shot at getting an athletic scholarship. Scouts don't look at losing teams."

His youngest brother sighed. "We didn't have a shot before you. We know there are no guarantees."

"You can't count on being an athlete," Brooks agreed. "You need an education, too. You have to have a career plan in place."

Brad laughed. "You sound just like Miss Pr— Miss Andrews."

Ryan snorted with disgust. "She got to you."

Brooks was afraid that she had. But instead of admitting it, he changed the subject. "It's late, guys. You better hit the sack."

"Why do we have to go to bed? Dad's not home yet," Brad pointed out.

"Because you need your sleep," Brooks replied.

"We might actually get some tonight since Dad's leaving the kid at Myrtle's," Ryan said. "Too bad she couldn't stay there all the time."

Brad sighed. "Yeah, it's nice and quiet here."

Rubbing his throbbing forehead, Brooks murmured, "It is?"

"What are you going to do about her?" Ryan asked. "Her mom isn't coming back any more than our mom's coming back."

"So I keep her."

"But how?" Ryan asked. "If you really want to go back to playing, you'll have to leave Trout Creek. And she can't stay with us."

"I wouldn't do that." Their dad had raised enough kids on his own. "I guess I'll have to get a nanny for her."

"And drag them on the road with you?" Brad asked. "A baby going from city to city?"

The throbbing in his forehead increased in intensity. "I didn't really think it through," he admitted. He'd only just realized how empty the house felt with her gone.

"Have you thought about giving her up for adoption?" Brad asked.

"What?" His brother's question shocked Brooks. "You think that's okay?"

Ryan shrugged his broad shoulders. "Yeah. She's so little she won't remember you."

"I don't remember Mom at all," Brad said.

"Neither do I," Ryan agreed, "and I was about two. The baby would probably be happier with someone else, anyway."

"You don't think she's happy?" Brooks asked. If she wasn't—if he couldn't take care of her, he might have to consider giving her up.

"Do you?" Ryan looked skeptical. "She cries all the time."

"Newborns cry." He'd been reading books and talking to Myrtle and the school nurse, Trudy. "It doesn't mean she's not happy."

Ryan didn't seem convinced. "Maybe not. But she'd probably be happier with someone who really wants her. You could find her a good home."

"I could," he agreed. "And I will if I decide she'd be better off with someone else. But first I have to find her mother." But he couldn't remember the names of women he'd dated nearly a year ago. Hell, he could barely remember the names of the ones he'd dated weeks ago.

But he knew there was one woman he wouldn't be able to forget, even when he left Trout Creek. Priscilla...

Chapter Twelve

"I can't believe you're letting me drive all the way to the city," Maureen said as she pressed her foot harder on the accelerator. "You don't even like riding with me to school."

"That's because you drive too fast."

But apparently her sister wasn't the only one in their family who moved too quickly. What had she been thinking, to make love with Brooks?

Of course, the answer was she hadn't been thinking.

"I can drive after I make a call," she said as she dug inside her purse for a business card.

"Who are you calling?"

"I'm returning a call." Margaret Everly had left a message on Priscilla's machine that she needed to speak with her, probably about the way the media had descended on Trout Creek and particularly on the Hoover household. But Trout Creek had closed ranks on the outsiders to protect Faith. No one was talking about the baby left on his doorstep.

"Brooks?" Maureen asked. "Did he call you?"

"No," she replied. He hadn't called her since that night they'd made love. Actually, he'd never called her before that, except to discuss the hockey team. And she hadn't expected him to start calling just because they'd had sex. She'd grown up listening to girls whine about Brooks never calling. And she'd felt all smug and superior because she hadn't been interested in him.

Then.

Now she couldn't stop thinking about him, couldn't stop thinking about all those wonderful things he'd said to her. About her being special. Beautiful. About how he'd wanted to listen to her.

But how could he listen if they never talked?

Fingers snapped in front of her face. "You okay?" Maureen asked.

Priscilla nodded.

"It'll get better."

She flinched, remembering when her sister had last made that claim to her—after they'd buried Courtney.

"Well, not from Stan's perspective," Maureen continued, amending her statement. "He's going to miss the money from having those reporters filling up the lodge. They all checked out this morning. I think they got sick of hearing how great and wonderful Brooks Hoover is."

"They're not the only ones," she remarked.

"You drank the Kool-Aid, too," Maureen reminded her with a chuckle. Then she primly recited, "'We're lucky to have Mr. Hoover coaching our hockey team this season.'"

Priscilla bit her lip, holding in a laugh over her

sister's prissy imitation of her. From working with teenagers, she knew not to encourage their childish behavior.

"You'd be luckier if you just *had* Brooks," Maureen remarked, then gave a wolfish whistle. "I could never understand why you didn't have a crush on him growing up. I was a lot older and still thought he was adorable. Then. Now." She whistled again.

Priscilla shook her head. "You're incorrigible." And that was why she could never share what had happened with Brooks with her sister or anyone else.

"And you're boring. You need to live a little. Have some fun."

Priscilla shifted uncomfortably as she remembered how much fun she'd had with Brooks.

"I'll have fun at the mall," she promised, "once I make this call." She pulled the social worker's card from her purse and punched in the woman's office number. Margaret Everly had left her cell number on Priscilla's machine, but she might pick up that phone.

"So are you calling Brooks?"

"No. And you're starting to act like the kids you serve lunch to," she accused.

"Hey—"

Priscilla held up a finger as the answering service picked up. After the beep, she said, "Mrs. Everly, I'm sorry. I know I assured you that I'd check in on the Hoovers. But I don't really feel that I can be objective about them. From everything I've seen, Faith is being taken care of very well. If you need any other information, you should really talk to the Hoovers directly."

Maureen shook her head, disgusted. "You were spying for the social worker?"

Priscilla sighed. "Yes. But not anymore."

"Why not?" her sister asked. "Change of heart?"

She hoped like hell that wasn't the case. No way did she want Brooks Hoover to have an effect on her heart.

"WHERE'S MISS PR— ANDREWS?" Brad asked, glancing up at the empty stands of the Icehouse. "She's usually here spying on us."

"She's not spying, she's supervising," Brooks said in her defense. "And I'm sure she had other things to do today." Like avoiding him. No doubt she considered the other night a mistake. So did he, despite—or maybe because of—how amazing making love with her had been. She was too distracting. The last few nights Faith had spent at Myrtle's, but still Brooks hadn't slept.

He wanted to blame his uncertain future for keeping him awake. Or the tough challenges he'd taken on. But it was Priscilla's face that he'd seen every time he'd closed his eyes.

"Coach!" Wes called out, impatient for the next play.

He forced his focus back on his team. "Okay, guys, you're looking better out there." Safer. One good thing to come of the leaked footage was that the helmet straps were always tightly clasped now.

"We're better because we got Erik back," Brad remarked. "It's cool that Miss Pr—Miss Andrews lifted his suspension."

Maybe between Erik and Ryan defending the net, no

shots would get through to the goalie. But Brooks couldn't play both boys every minute of every period, not unless he wanted to damage their bodies. "We need to discuss the game we played earlier this week," he said, turning his attention to Wes. "We have to cut down on the penalties."

"We gotta be slicker, so the refs don't catch us?" Brad asked.

Brooks grimaced. That was the way he'd played. Fast and aggressive and, when the game had been too close, dirty. "No, we gotta play cleaner."

"But you've spent a lot of time in the penalty box," Ryan scoffed.

He knew his brothers would call him on any hypocrisy. "But that doesn't make me a badass. It makes me an idiot for handing the other team a chance to score on a power play." That was how the Trout Creek High team had lost their first game of the season.

"We need a better goalie," Brad said, shooting a glare at Adam. "Then they wouldn't be able to score on the power play."

"Hey, look who's here!" Ryan shouted.

Brooks turned toward the stands again, searching for Priscilla—hopeful that she'd changed her mind. It used to annoy him when she'd showed up to watch, because he figured she didn't trust him. Now he missed her. He scanned the bleachers for her.

But their visitor walked onto the ice.

"Hey, D., you gonna play?" Ryan asked Debbie, his voice cracking with excitement. "Adam sucks in the net. We need you out there!"

"He's right," Brooks added. "We really do need you back on the team."

"I know," she said matter-of-factly.

"Are you ready to come back?" he asked.

She shrugged shoulders nearly as broad as Ryan's. "I'm not sure I should," she said with a glance toward that particular player. "I really want to focus on my grades."

But she'd been drawn back to the ice.

"I give the guys study time," Brooks said, an initiative he'd just started after learning Brad was doing Ryan's homework. "We even have tutoring."

"Me," Brad said with a snort. "I'm the tutor."

Debbie nodded. "That's cool." She glanced around the stands. "Where's the baby? I hear that you sometimes bring her to practice."

"Just once," he said, flinching at the memory. It was a wonder Priscilla hadn't called the social worker on him. "I didn't know that Buzz doesn't use the heat much anymore."

And Brooks had figured out why; the old man could barely afford to run the arena. Brooks would hate to see the Trout Creek Icehouse shut down. But he couldn't imagine who would buy the money pit. With the economy in the toilet, hardly anyone could afford to pay for ice time anymore.

"I can watch her sometime," she offered. "If you want me to…"

He didn't want to hurt the girl's feelings, but he preferred to have someone older watch Faith—like Myrtle. Or Priscilla.

But the expression on Priscilla's face every time she looked at the baby was so wistful, so pained, that it reached deep inside Brooks. It affected him as not much else ever had. *She* affected him.

"I'm cutting back on my shifts at the store," Debbie added. "So I can be available."

"I'd rather have you as a goalie," he persisted. "Would you consider coming back?"

Debbie glanced again at the ice, and she wore that expression of longing Priscilla had when she looked at Faith.

He needed to talk to her again. No, he needed to follow through on his promise to just listen. There was more to that look than her failed marriage. But even if he learned what it was, he doubted he could help her get over it. He already had more responsibility than he could handle.

He was the one who faced failure now. At fatherhood, at being a coach. And it wasn't just Trout Creek watching him. The reporters had been at the kids' game, recording his defeat. He'd caught a bit of the coverage. Someone had remarked that the prize-winning fish mounted on the walls of the Trout Creek Inn would have done a better job coaching and playing. The fish showed more life.

"You love the game, Debbie," he reminded the girl.

"Yes," she admitted, but she wasn't staring at the ice. She was ogling his clueless brother. She definitely had it bad.

But Ryan was too much like him: shallow and self-absorbed. Just as Brooks had never noticed how special and beautiful Priscilla was back in school, neither would Ryan realize that Debbie was more than a great goalie.

But Brooks couldn't think of any advice for the girl. He knew nothing about teenage relationships. Hell, he didn't know anything about adult relationships. All he knew was hockey. Playing it.

Maybe he should stop wasting his time in Trout Creek and try to get back in the game himself. He could talk to some neuro specialists and figure out if he had a future on the ice.

And if he didn't, then he'd have to figure out a future off the ice. Hell, maybe he could identify with these teenagers more than he'd realized. Just like them, he needed to figure out what he wanted to do with the rest of his life.

Chapter Thirteen

Priscilla winced at the deafening volume of the music and the blinding flash of the strobe lights. She could only imagine Brooks's headache. The decorating committee had gone a little overboard. But then there was so little to do in Trout Creek that every sport and every dance had more importance than in other cities, like the one where Priscilla had previously worked.

Maureen, standing next to her in her new yellow pantsuit, gestured at the girls' dresses. The silks and chiffons, some floor length, would have been more appropriate for a prom. In the city, the girls had worn cocktail length or shorter outfits for homecoming.

Shouting to be heard over the music, her sister asked, "Aren't you glad I talked you into that new dress?"

"I know I am," Brooks said, coming up to join them. His dark eyes gleamed with appreciation and his usual mischief as his gaze traveled up from her black sandals, over her legs to the low bodice of the green dress.

Priscilla felt the sudden urge to tug up the neckline. She shouldn't have listened to Maureen, who insisted it was demure enough for the assistant principal. Because there was nothing demure about the heat streaking through her.

Of course, that might have more to do with Brooks. He'd done as she'd asked and worn a dark suit with a crisp white shirt that set off the remnants of his summer tan. The tie seemed to be a problem, though. It looped around his neck undone.

"Do you need help with that?" Maureen offered.

Disappointment flashed through Priscilla that her sister had beaten her to the task, but then she felt Maureen's hand on the small of her back. "Help the man out," she ordered, shoving her close to Brooks, before slipping off through the crowd.

Priscilla forced a smile. "Subtle, huh?"

"Just like my dad when he wants his way," Brooks agreed with a grin. "But I could use a hand."

Heart pounding hard, she reached for the silver silk. Drawing her bottom lip between her teeth, she concentrated on tying the tie. As she tightened the knot, his throat rippled with a deep swallow. "Too tight?" she asked.

"Just right." But when his pupils dilated, she knew he was talking about something else entirely.

"You look so beautiful," he murmured. "Green is my favorite color."

She smiled with amusement. He was trying to charm her again. "That's because it's your team color."

He shook his head and stepped closer, sliding his fingers across her cheek. "It's because of your eyes."

She released a shaky breath she'd meant as a laugh.

But she couldn't laugh when her pulse was racing with excitement. She brushed his hand away from her face and glanced around to see if anyone was watching them. Well, besides Maureen.

They seemed to be attracting too much attention.

"You need to behave," she admonished him.

He grinned. "You know I'm a bad boy."

She shook her head. "No, that's just what you want everyone to think." So that they wouldn't expect much from him.

"Don't believe my press," he warned her. "It's only good right now thanks to my baby brother's spin. And your interview. You blew your chance to set the record straight about who actually made the mistake of hiring me."

"Correction," she admonished. "It was my mistake not to give you a chance."

"Yeah, right. We lost our game the other night."

"That was just the first scrimmage," she reminded him. "And you showed promise." Not just the team but him.

"So you saw the game?"

"I was there," she admitted.

"I didn't see you."

She'd made certain he hadn't. No way did she want him to think that she expected more from him personally.

"It's my job to be there," she reminded him.

"You haven't stopped by to watch a practice in days," he said. "I've missed you."

"I've been busy with homecoming and Halloween next week." And trying to avoid him so she wouldn't think about their night together and want more.

"You can't avoid me tonight," he warned her.

Someone called out her name, and she smiled at Brooks. "Wanna bet?" she teased before heading off into the crowd of teenagers.

Most of the night passed in a blur—consoling heart-broken girls, guarding the punch bowl and separating overamorous couples. And every time Priscilla passed her sister, she glared at her for talking her into buying heels that had her feet aching.

Every time she passed Brooks, her heart ached with longing. As she passed the punch bowl again, he caught her hand and entwined their fingers. "Come dance with me."

Twelve years ago, she might have been thrilled if he'd asked her to dance at their homecoming. But now she didn't want her students watching and wondering what was going on between her and Brooks. Hell, she wouldn't have wanted that in high school, either. She had been a smart girl—a good girl. She shook her head and planted her heels, refusing to be tugged onto the floor with the gyrating couples. "No, we're supposed to be chaperoning."

"Chaperones can't dance?" he asked. He pointed toward the floor. "I think they could probably use a chaperone out there more than here on the sidelines."

When Priscilla glanced at the dancers again, he pulled her out on the gym floor. As if he'd given a cue to the DJ, a slow song started to play, and Brooks wrapped his arms around her. She could have just stood there, stiff and tense in his embrace, but that might draw more attention.

Not that everyone wasn't already watching them. She glimpsed her sister, grinning. When he spun her around, Priscilla noticed two students in particular. Brooks's brothers were staring at them, but they weren't smiling.

"See, it was a good idea to come out here," Brooks said, his mouth close to her ear.

Her heart thumped hard against her ribs. "This was *not* a good idea," she argued, surreptitiously wedging some space between them before she melted into the hard muscles of his chest.

"Why not?" he asked. "We're both out here doing our job."

She didn't dare glance at the kids on the floor for fear they would realize how turned on she was. "We are?"

"Sure, it's a great spot to watch them. You can make sure everyone keeps their hands where you can see 'em." His palm skimmed down her back to the curve of her hip. The heat of his touch penetrated the thin material of her dress, making her want nothing between them.

She caught his wrist and tugged on it to lead him off to the side of the floor. Dancing with him had been a very bad idea. "I'm more worried about your hands."

"Hey, I've gotta prove I deserve that bad-boy reputation," he teased, that mischievous glint as bright as the strobe lights.

"I knew I shouldn't have asked you to come," she said. "That I'd wind up chaperoning you."

"Then why *did* you ask?"

She shot a glare in her sister's direction. "Maureen

talked me into—" Her sister was waving her arms wildly, gesturing for them to come quickly. "Come on, she needs us."

Priscilla rushed off, half hoping that Brooks would not follow as she pushed through the crowd.

"What's going on?" she asked Maureen. Or had her sister just picked up that Priscilla needed an excuse for some distance from Brooks?

"What's up?" he asked from behind her.

"There's a fight," Maureen replied.

"Where?" Priscilla asked.

"Boys' bathroom."

Priscilla started in that direction, but Brooks tugged her back, his hand entwined with hers again. "I've got this," he said. "It's the boys' bathroom. And I don't think Mr. Drover can handle a fight."

He couldn't handle anything from home, which was exactly where the principal had decided to spend the evening. "I'm the assistant principal," she reminded Brooks. "I can go in the boys' bathroom."

"One of you better go before they kill each other," Maureen urged. But as Priscilla started forward again, her sister grabbed her arm. "Let Brooks handle it."

"But it's my job." And the only thing she'd ever been really good at.

"You take too much on yourself." Her sister was in mother mode again. "He can handle a little fight on his own. He's good with those kids. You stay here and I'll grab you some cold punch. I know if I'd been dancing with Brooks Hoover I'd need some cooling off."

The minute her sister walked away, Priscilla fanned

herself with her hand. She hoped no one had noticed how much Brooks had affected her. But she wasn't only worried about her chances of taking over Mr. Drover's job one day. She was worried that Brooks knew how much she wanted him.

She glanced around. Fewer couples crowded the dance floor now. More students gathered in the hall outside the bathroom where the fight raged. With a sigh, she headed toward the action. She didn't doubt that Brooks would be able to break up the boys, but it was her job to dole out the punishment: suspension for fighting.

Before she could walk through the doors of the gym, someone caught her arm. "Miss Andrews, uh, can we talk a minute?"

Surprised, she turned toward Ryan Hoover. In a dark suit, the boy was nearly as handsome as his older brother. "So you're not one of the boys in the bathroom?" she teased.

He didn't realize she was joking because his face tensed and paled. "'Course you'd think I was causing trouble. If something goes wrong, you always blame a Hoover."

"Most of the time I'd be right," she reminded him. But neither he nor Brad had committed any serious offenses, nothing like the kids at the previous school where she'd worked. Skipping classes, cheating on tests and TPing her house were probably the extent of their crimes.

"You're not always right," he said.

She glanced toward the hall. The crowd stepped back as Brooks emerged from the bathroom. He had his arms around two teenagers. Fortunately, the kids were no longer swinging at each other. Instead they shook hands, at Brooks's urging. That might be how he handled violence on the ice, but she needed to talk to those kids. With Brooks in the way, she couldn't immediately identify them.

Ryan stepped between her and the scene, drawing her attention back to him.

"No, I'm not always right," she agreed. She had been so certain that Brooks would have been a bad influence on the kids.

"You are right about him," Ryan said somberly.

Startled, Priscilla turned fully toward the boy. As loyal as the Hoovers were to each other, she had to have misunderstood. "What do you mean?"

"You shouldn't have hired him," Ryan said.

She could have pointed out that she hadn't, that his father had gone over her head to Principal Drover. But instead she said, "You wanted him as your coach! You TP'd my house when you believed I hadn't hired him."

"I hadn't thought it through—what it would be like having my big brother as my coach." He lifted his broad shoulders in a sheepish shrug.

"Do you think he's too hard on you?" Coming from a professional league, maybe Brooks expected too much of a high school team. She'd watched his practices, though, and hadn't noticed any undue pressure. But that had been before the media had found out he was coaching. Now the whole country had an eye on him.

Ryan shook his head. "He's not as hard as Coach Cook. He wants to make sure we don't get hurt."

"So he's too soft?" She glanced around, wishing Brad would join them. The youngest Hoover often had to translate for his less articulate brother.

"Nah, it's not about his coaching. He's a good coach." There was the famous Hoover loyalty she'd thought he lacked.

"Then I don't understand," she said, summoning her patience when she really wanted to corral the boys who'd been fighting. But she doubted she would have an opportunity for an open discussion with Ryan again. "Why shouldn't I have hired him?"

"Because you knew he wouldn't stick around."

Dread almost overwhelmed her. "He's leaving?"

"Not yet, but he will," the kid said with total certainty. "Once he's cleared to play again he'll be taking off."

"But he has the baby now," she reminded him. "What will he do with her?"

He shrugged. "I don't know. But if her mom doesn't come back, I think he's gonna give her up for adoption."

"He would do that?" He would give away a baby? She'd wanted hers so badly and hadn't been able to keep her. Tears threatened, but she blinked fast, refusing to let them sting, let alone fall.

"He's not a dad," Ryan said.

"But he spends so much time with her. He seems to care about her." He'd given her a name.

"And that's probably why he'll give her up. He knows himself. Hell—heck, you know him. You knew him for a long time. Did you ever think he'd be a dad?"

"No," she admitted.

"He's not a coach, either," Ryan said.

"But you said that he's a good coach," she reminded him.

"He's a good coach, but he's a great player," Ryan explained. Maybe Brad wasn't the smarter one of the two. This Hoover had more going on than he had allowed anyone to believe. "Brooks needs to be playing."

"I know that," she admitted.

He wouldn't care about Faith or Priscilla in the way they deserved to be loved. Just like when he'd been a kid, all he cared about was hockey.

"Good." Ryan sighed, his shoulders drooping as if the tension had eased from them. He had really been worried about his older brother. She suspected he idolized the man. "I thought you might think he was gonna stick around, that he might be the guy...you know."

"The guy?"

"The guy for you."

She laughed, not at him but at her own foolishness. For just a little bit she had entertained the silly dream that the two of them could be more than boss and employee, more than old schoolmates. She assured his brother and reminded herself, "Brooks Hoover is definitely not the guy for me."

BROOKS SUCKED IN a breath of surprise. He'd seen Priscilla in deep conversation with Ryan and had wanted to know what they were talking about. But that would teach him for eavesdropping, because as the old saying claimed, you never heard anything good about yourself. Hell, a month ago, he would have been relieved to learn that Priscilla had no illusions about him.

Even now he should be relieved that she'd woven no romantic fantasies of happily ever after with him. He had decided long ago that, given his genes, he wasn't capable of it.

Priscilla's brow furrowed as she stared at him, probably trying to figure out if she'd hurt his feelings or not. He grinned, trying to assure her that her remark was no big deal.

"Where are the fighters?" she asked.

"Maureen's getting 'em ice packs."

"Are they in the kitchen, then? I need to talk to them."

"Wh-why?" Ryan asked, grabbing her arm again. "Brooks broke up the fight. It's over."

She turned to his brother, her expression suspicious. She must have caught on, as he just had, that Ryan was trying to run interference. "What's going on here? It's almost as if nobody wants me to see who was fighting."

"Because we don't," Brooks admitted.

"I need to know," she insisted, her face flushing with indignation. "Fighting on school grounds means an automatic suspension." She nodded as if she'd answered her own question. "And from after-school sports teams."

"Can't you just bend the rule this one time?" Ryan implored her.

She glanced from Brooks to Ryan and back again. "I now know who one of them is."

Brooks pushed his hand through his hair. "My most critical player."

"If you suspend him, we'll have to forfeit every game," Ryan said. "We won't even be able to play."

And with nothing to do, Brooks would have no reason to stay in Trout Creek.

Chapter Fourteen

For once Brooks didn't stumble over the shoes in the foyer. Someone had actually put them away in the seldom-used hall closet. Since Faith had come into their lives, Myrtle had been around more often to clean, and his dad was making the boys pick up after themselves, too.

The first thing Brooks did was check the bassinet in his bedroom. She was back, the tiny pink bundle who had turned his life upside down. She'd been with Myrtle for a few days, and the house was eerily quiet even with teenage boys. How would he just give the baby up? Even if it was best for her, as his brothers had suggested?

He didn't think he could be that selfless. Faith slept peacefully, but he doubted he would. Now he would never know if there was something he could have done if he couldn't play hockey. He'd never know if he would have been a good coach.

Instead of trying to sleep, he decided on television and a beer. But the family room was dark. The old man must have gone to bed after he'd put down the sleeping baby. So Brooks flipped the light switch.

Two bodies sprang apart on the sofa, one rolling onto the floor with a bang and an oath.

"Damn!" Brooks turned away from more skin than he'd ever wanted to see—his father's and Myrtle's. "Sorry," he mumbled, backing toward the door, his face hot with embarrassment.

"Damn," Rex muttered.

"I didn't mean to barge in on…" His worst nightmare. No one wanted to catch his parent like that. But in a way, it was good to know the old man had a personal life, that he hadn't stopped living after his wife left him. He'd found a really nice, trustworthy woman this time.

Brooks headed into his room. But before he could close the door—and gouge out his eyeballs at what he'd seen—his dad stepped inside with him.

"Sorry you, uh, walked in on that," Rex murmured, his face flaming red.

"You're lucky it was me and not the boys."

"They called and said they had to take care of something. So I extended their curfew for an hour."

Take care of something? Brooks hoped they'd given their dad more of an explanation than that.

"And I thought you'd be out late with Miss Andrews," his dad continued.

"Why would you think that? We weren't on a date. I was just a chaperone." A grin tugged at his lips. "I didn't think I would need to chaperone at home, too." He hadn't wanted young babysitters because he'd worried about his brothers distracting them from taking care of Faith. He hadn't thought he had to worry about his dad.

"Uh, we've been seeing each other for a while now," his father admitted.

Brooks nodded. He remembered Myrtle helping him care for another baby—Brad. Back then Brooks had just thought she'd been chipping in like everyone else in Trout Creek. "For a long while now."

Rex nodded in turn.

"And Mom's been gone even longer," Brooks said. It was well past time that his father moved on. "I think Myrtle is great."

His dad grinned with a happiness Brooks could never remember seeing on the old man's face before. "Yeah, I think she's pretty great, too."

For the first time since awakening from that coma, Brooks reached out to his father and squeezed his shoulder. "I'm happy for you."

"You know who else I think is great?"

Brooks glanced toward his sleeping daughter. "Yeah, Grandpa?"

"Well, Faith, of course," he said. "But I was actually talking about Priscilla Andrews."

Brooks laughed. "Yeah, right."

"No, really. I think she's a wonderful young woman."

"When did you come to that conclusion?" he asked wryly. "The first time she suspended Ryan? Or when she refused to hire me?"

"I didn't say I always agree with her." Rex grinned. "But she's smart. And strong."

Brooks studied his father. Once again he suspected the old man knew what had brought Priscilla home to Trout Creek. But Brooks didn't want to hear it from him; he wanted to hear it from her.

"She's independent," Brooks added. "Self-reliant. That's what you need to be teaching the boys."

"What do you mean?"

"Stop cleaning up their messes for them," he said in response. Faith murmured in her sleep just then and let out a wistful little sigh. "And for me..."

"You're going to be able to do that, you think?" Grandpa stepped closer to the bassinet and adjusted the light blanket over the baby's tiny shoulders. "You're going to be able to let her get hurt and not do anything to try to fix it?"

Brooks gazed down at the sleeping baby. "No. But they have got to grow up sometime. I have to grow up sometime."

"So grow up," his dad told him.

"That means making my own decisions," Brooks warned him. "About playing." After tonight, his coaching job was probably over anyway. "About staying." He stared down at the baby. "About Faith."

"Mrs. Everly stopped by tonight."

He groaned, regretting that he'd been out. "She did? And I missed her?"

"It was an unannounced visit, so she could check up on us."

"She didn't surprise you like I did...?"

The old man laughed. "No, she was here much earlier. She said that Miss Andrews had been keeping an eye on things for her and that she was sure you were doing a great job with Faith."

"What!" So Priscilla had been spying on him.

"But since Priscilla told her she couldn't check on you anymore, Mrs. Everly needed to make an official visit herself."

"So Priscilla quit?"

"Yup, but she assured the social worker you were doing fine."

He wasn't fine. And he suspected that neither was she right now.

HEARING THE ENGINE outside the cabin, Priscilla grimaced. She would probably awaken to more toilet paper streamers hanging from her trees come morning. But she wasn't so sure who'd be doing the TPing this time. She stepped closer to the window and peered out—right into a man's eyes. A scream slipped through her lips, but it wasn't loud enough for anyone to hear her up at the lodge. No one could protect her from this man.

Her hand shaking, Priscilla opened the door. Brooks still wore his dark suit, and she wore her dress, although she'd kicked off those merciless shoes.

"I know you're mad," she said. "Go ahead and yell. I won't bend the rule about the suspension."

"Not even for Adam?" Brooks asked as he stepped inside. Instead of being angry, he seemed almost sympathetic. "He's your nephew."

She sighed. "I know. Believe me, I know. Maureen's been yelling at me. In fact she's probably out there helping your brothers TP my trees."

He laughed. "I didn't see anyone."

"You'd lie for them," she said. "You must be mad, too. I had to suspend Adam and Wes. I can't believe Adam got in a fight." She'd thought for certain she would find Brad in the kitchen with an ice pack on his eye. Instead it had been her sweet, easygoing nephew.

"I gotta admit I've wanted to punch Wes a time or two myself," Brooks confessed. "The kid could provoke a nun to violence."

"But I can't *not* punish Adam," she persisted. "He broke a rule."

"He's my only goalie. I can't put anyone else in the net. We'll have to forfeit the season."

"Will you leave?" she asked with a certain amount of dread as she remembered his brother's warning. And now he wouldn't have a job.

He lifted his shoulders in a shrug, but his dark gaze caught hers and held. "I don't know if I have a reason to stay."

She swallowed hard. "Faith?"

"Faith in my team? Adam wasn't a good goalie, but he was better than no goalie."

"I meant Faith, your daughter."

He nodded. "I know. You thought I forgot her again—like at the restaurant that day."

"Could you forget about her? If you gave her up?" Priscilla had worried about growing too attached, because she was certain the little girl's mother would return to claim her. But of course Brooks had other options than single parenthood.

"Ryan told you?"

"He was trying to stall, so he was rambling. I wasn't sure if it was true or not." Until now. She glimpsed the turmoil in Brooks's eyes. But was it over giving Faith up or keeping her?

"I don't know if I could do it." He pushed a hand through his disheveled curls. "I just don't know. Her mom hasn't turned up. You'd think that if she saw the press about me, she would contact me to find out why the baby wasn't mentioned. She was able to do it—to just walk away and not look back. Like my mom."

He was afraid, Priscilla realized. Worried that he was like his mother. "I wasn't able to…" She swallowed the lump of emotion that rushed up. "I wasn't able to forget."

"Priscilla?" He flinched, as if he felt her pain. "What are you saying?"

"I had a baby, too."

"Oh my God. I didn't know. Nobody's said anything. Did you have to give her up?"

Priscilla blinked, fighting back tears. "No. I lost her."

"Oh my God!" He stepped closer and slid his arms around her, as if he could absorb her pain. "She died?"

"Courtney." Her voice cracked as she said her baby's name aloud for the first time in years. "She was eight weeks old. She died from meningitis. She just got so sick, so fast. There was nothing the doctors could do for her. They told me there was nothing I could have done."

"But you didn't believe them?"

"No." She struggled for breath as sobs racked her. "And neither did Owen."

"Owen?"

"My ex."

"The son of a bitch." Brooks cursed. "How dare he—"

"He never said it. But I saw it in his eyes every time he looked at me. The blame. I couldn't stand him looking at me. So I just left." And divorce papers had followed her not long after she'd settled back in Trout Creek.

"He was wrong," Brooks said, easing away to gently cup her face in his palms. He tipped her chin up, so she had to meet his gaze. "He was wrong to blame you for something that wasn't your fault. And he was wrong to let you go."

"It's not fair," she murmured, the tears falling. It wasn't fair that her baby had died. And it wasn't fair that Brooks Hoover was being so sweet, so wonderful, that she found herself falling for him.

"I know," he agreed. He held her close again, his arms tight around her. "I'm so sorry. And so insensitive. I never should have asked you to watch Faith."

"No, you shouldn't have trusted me," she agreed.

He eased back, his hands gripping her shoulders. "Damn it, woman. You know you weren't to blame. There's no way you would let a child come to harm. Faith was safe and secure with you. But it must have been hard for you to see her, to hold her…"

Priscilla nodded. "At first. But then it got easier."

"I saw your face. I knew you were hurting." His voice was thick with self-disgust.

"It's okay," she assured him. "You didn't know. No one but my family does."

"I'm glad you told me," he said.

She hadn't wanted to, hadn't wanted him any closer than she'd already let him, especially now, when she knew he wouldn't stay. But she'd also wanted him to realize how hard it would be for him to give up Faith.

"Is that why you agreed to spy on us for Mrs. Everly?" he asked. "To make sure Faith was okay?"

She tensed. "You know?"

"My dad told me."

"Of course." There was nothing the sheriff didn't know. "I shouldn't have agreed to it, but you've kept her safe." More than she'd done for her baby.

"Oh, Priscilla, I'm so sorry…."

She shook her head and fought back the emotions rushing up to choke her. "It happened a long time ago."

"But you still hurt. I've seen it so many times in your eyes."

She was sick of hurting. Sick of living in the past and planning for the future. She wanted only the present. Only Brooks. She hooked her arms behind his neck and pulled his head down for her kiss. As perceptive as ever, he must have understood how badly she needed him. His mouth pressed hard against hers, parting her lips. His tongue slid inside, driving deep, while his hands fisted in her dress.

Priscilla moaned. She lifted her legs and wrapped them tight around his waist. He carried her the few paces across the small living room to her bedroom, where he laid her on the bed and followed her down.

His erection pressed against her hips, and she arched into him. He groaned and pulled his mouth from hers. "It's been killing me. Wanting you like this again."

"Me, too."

"We can keep this fun," he said, but no glint of mischief brightened his serious gaze. "We can keep this light."

She nodded in agreement because she couldn't speak the lie aloud. She was not the type who could make love with a man without having deeper feelings for him than friendship. And she was definitely falling for Brooks.

But as his fingers moved over her, sliding down the straps of her homecoming dress and caressing her shoulders, she didn't care. She reached up and undid the tie she'd knotted for him earlier that evening.

"I imagined you doing this, taking off my tie," he said, his voice gruff with passion, "after the dance."

"Me, too," she admitted. She pulled the silk free of his collar and dropped it next to the bed. Then she fumbled with the buttons of his shirt to bare the hard muscles of his chest. She arched up and skimmed her lips across him, feeling his heart rate kick up. If only she could affect his heart that easily…

But he wasn't staying in Trout Creek. Even without his brother's warning, she'd known that. So she had to make the most of the time they had.

She pressed her palms against his chest, gliding them over the muscles there. And she shifted closer, sliding her leg over his thighs. Beneath the fly of his dress pants, his erection hardened and pulsed, and she rubbed against him. Her dress rode up around her waist, so she felt him through the thin material of her panties. She moved against him again, heat pooling between her legs.

He groaned. "Priscilla…"

She kissed him quickly, intimately, then pulled back. "What do you see in my eyes now?"

"Need."

The revelation shook her. She'd expected him to say desire, or passion. But he was right. She needed him. "Make love to me."

"With you," he corrected, as he reached behind her and tugged down her zipper.

The dress dropped to her waist, her breasts spilling over the strapless bra. Then it was gone, too. And his mouth was there, sliding over the curve of her breasts, dipping between them before his lips closed around a nipple. With his tongue he teased the sensitive point.

She arched her back, and pressure began to build inside her, tightening her muscles. Tangling her fingers in his hair, she clutched him to her breast.

He pulled back to strip off her dress and silk panties, and his mouth moved down her body, from her breast to her navel and the place where the tension wound tightest. He kissed her there, as intimately as he'd kissed her lips, and his tongue slid inside her.

She gasped and lifted off the bed, meeting the thrusts of his tongue…until the pressure broke and an orgasm shuddered through her. She cried out. The rasp of his zipper echoed the sound as he dropped his pants. A crinkling of foil, and he was sheathed in latex and then her body.

"You're so big," she murmured.

But then he rolled so she was on top. She took him deeper and he grasped her hips, helping her move up and down, backward and forward. All the while thrusting deeper inside her.

His hands moved back up her body, cupping her

breasts. His thumbs rubbed across the sensitive points and he took one in his mouth.

The pressure, which had built again, broke free as another powerful orgasm shattered Priscilla. Brooks kept pushing her down and pulling her up until he tensed and shouted her name. His body, so muscular and strong, shuddered beneath her. "Damn…"

"Damn," she echoed.

"I let you distract me," he said, breathing hard.

"That's what that was?" she asked with a smile. "A distraction?"

"I want to talk."

"Why do I suspect that's something you've never said to a naked woman before?" she teased.

She was right, Brooks acknowledged. But Priscilla was different. He lifted her off him so she wouldn't distract him again, since he was already hardening inside her wet heat.

"We're going to talk," he insisted. But when he came back from the bathroom, the bedroom was empty. He picked up his clothes from the floor, pulled on his pants and shrugged into his shirt, not bothering with the buttons. He found her in the living room, in a robe, standing before the windows.

"Do you think they're out there?" she asked.

"The boys?" He shrugged. "I doubt it. They know I'll make them clean up whatever they do."

"That does kind of take the fun out of it," she agreed, and turned to him with a pointed look.

He understood what she was really saying. "Like talking would take the fun out of…"

"This," she said. "We don't need to talk about anything. It's not like we have a future."

He should have been relieved that she didn't want more from him than he was sure he could offer, but instead he sucked in a breath as if she'd jabbed an elbow in his ribs. "We're friends, though, right?"

"Yes." She laughed. "That was something I never thought I'd say twelve years ago."

"I was a jerk back then. But I'm trying now. I want to be a friend. So talk to me. Tell me about your marriage," he urged.

She looked hesitant. "Like I said, it was a long time ago. It doesn't matter anymore."

He stepped closer and skimmed his thumb along her jaw. "Liar."

"I had just graduated college and started my first job when I discovered I was a pregnant."

"You weren't married?" he asked, with surprise but no condemnation. He was the last person who could judge someone.

"Owen and I had dated all through college."

"So you were serious?"

"I was," she said. "I don't think he was—at least not as much as me. He probably wouldn't have married me if I hadn't gotten pregnant. But he wanted to do the right thing, so he proposed." Her voice sounded shaky.

The son of a bitch had really hurt her, made her feel unloved and undeserving. "He was an idiot," Brooks said.

"For doing the right thing?"

"For not marrying you for *you*."

She shrugged. "In the end it didn't matter. Once we lost Courtney, we had no reason to stay married."

Brooks pulled her back into his arms. "I'm sorry."

"It was a long time ago," she repeated, but tears penetrated his shirt. She dashed them away and stepped back. "I'm okay, friend."

"Friend," he repeated with resignation.

"That's really all we can be," she said.

"Yes," he agreed with a sigh.

She had already been hurt by one man who hadn't known what he wanted. Until he figured out his own life, Brooks had nothing to offer her.

Chapter Fifteen

Months had passed, the holidays coming and going, and still Brooks had not left Trout Creek. Priscilla didn't kid herself into thinking he had stuck around for her. It was his love of the game.

Instead of TPing her trees that night after the homecoming dance, his brothers had talked Debbie into playing again. And with a complete team to coach, Brooks had taken his new responsibilities seriously. She could barely hear her own thoughts over the roar of the cheering crowd in the ice arena.

Fingers clutched her arm, digging through the down of her heavy jacket to shake her. "They're winning!" Maureen screamed. "They're amazing!"

After sitting out a month's suspension, Adam was playing again, passing the puck back to Brad. Maureen had come along as a chaperone for the away game, as well as to cheer her son.

The Trout Creek team was playing in a tournament downstate, just an hour north of the city where Brooks had played before he'd been injured. Most of his teammates, even the goalie who'd fought with him, had come out to support him despite having a game of their own that evening. They stood behind the glass, close to the bench where Brooks's high schoolers sat. Maybe the presence of his former teammates motivated the kids to play so hard, to do their coach proud. But then, they'd been playing this hard every game, winning all of them except the first one.

Another hand gripped Priscilla's shoulder and squeezed. When she turned on the bleachers to see who sat behind her, she was surprised to find Coach Cook. His eyes were bright with pride and excitement. "He's a damn good coach," he declared.

With no help from the cane hooked around his elbow, the older man stood up to cheer his granddaughter's save. The physical therapy was finally showing results.

After Priscilla sat back down, she leaned close to Maureen and asked, "Why did he tell me that Brooks is doing a good job?"

Did everyone know about the two of them? Probably. In Trout Creek everyone knew everyone else's business. But they'd tried to keep it quiet. Out in public they'd acted more like friends than lovers. Priscilla had insisted on that because she didn't want everyone feeling sorry for her when he left.

"You're his boss," her sister reminded her.

Heat rushed to Priscilla's face. "Of course. Yeah."

Coach Cook had just been letting her know she'd found a good replacement for him. Did he consider the position temporary? He was recovering from his stroke so quickly, he could likely return next season. And one season was really all Brooks had committed to. For now.

She couldn't accept Coach Cook's kudos for hiring Brooks, because she hadn't. If not for Sheriff Hoover's interference, Brooks would not be coach. Without him, she doubted the team would have made it to this tournament. She had been wrong about his coaching skills. Had she been wrong about him in regards to a relationship?

"You're not just his boss anymore, are you?" Maureen asked, her brow furrowed.

"No," she admitted, her voice pitched low enough that none of the other Trout Creek residents who'd traveled to the game could hear her. "We've taken things to a different level."

"How serious?"

"We're just having fun." She nearly choked on the last word. It was totally inadequate to describe the mind-blowing passion she felt whenever he touched her.

Her sister squeezed her arm again. "Oh, Priscilla…"

"I thought you'd be thrilled."

"I would be," Maureen said, "if I believed you were just having fun. But I know you, and I'm worried that you're going to get hurt."

"Maybe I won't this time," she said, but she heard the hollow ring of doubt in her own voice.

"It's not that he's a bad guy. In fact, I think he's too good."

Priscilla flinched at her sister's honesty. "Thanks."

"No, he's not too good for *you*," she hastened to explain. "I don't think there'll ever be a man good enough for you."

"Am I that hard to please?" It had never taken Brooks much to bring her pleasure. Just a kiss, a caress...

"That's not what I meant. It's just that Brooks Hoover is different," Maureen said, gesturing to where he stood with the benched members of his team.

As he spoke to them, they stared up at him with awe and adoration. But the kids weren't the only ones watching him. Cameras flashed, and it wasn't just parents taking pictures. The press had come, too—not to watch the kids play but to watch Brooks. His team's turnaround had renewed their interest in him. Just as his baby brother had promised, he was coaching his former team to glory.

"He's always been better than Trout Creek," Maureen explained. *"Bigger."*

Unable to argue, Priscilla nodded. He was talented and charming, but Brooks had greater depth than most people, including her, had realized.

"I always thought you were bigger than Trout Creek, too," her sister said with pride and perhaps some disappointment. "But you came back home a different person than the determined young woman who'd left."

She had come back wounded.

"I like my life in Trout Creek," she said defensively. She wasn't hiding. "It's home to me. Living somewhere else just convinced me that I belong there."

"Do you really think that Brooks does?" Maureen asked quietly.

"He's a good coach." But she remembered what Ryan had told her at the homecoming dance and what she had observed herself. "But he's a *great* player."

Next season he would return to his own team and the life he'd led before her or Faith. He would be training and playing long hours in different cities, with no time for the family Priscilla wanted. She deserved more—a man who'd love her and the children she now wanted more than anything else.

"He won't stay," her sister said bluntly.

"I know. That's why we're not serious. We're just having fun."

Shouts of joy and applause reverberated throughout the stands as Ryan assisted Brad to a goal, the winning goal as the last few seconds ran out on the clock. That clock was like her time with Brooks, running out all too fast.

OUTSIDE THE LOCKER ROOM, Graham slapped Brooks on the back. "You did a real good job with all those little smart-asses."

Bursting with pride, he grinned. "The little smart-asses are easier to work with than the big ones."

Graham had met Ryan and Brad, who hadn't been as forgiving as Brooks that Graham knocked their brother to the ice. But they couldn't have beaten up the man as much as he'd been beating up himself.

"I screwed up big-time," Graham said. "That girl was after whatever she could get. When I broke up with her, she sold that video she took with her cell phone to the highest bidder. I should have listened to you. Women can't be trusted."

Brooks had believed that once, because of his mom. But not since Priscilla. "I don't know about that."

"What?" Graham shook his head. "You told me some chick dropped a baby on your doorstep, and you're willing to trust another female?"

"Shh." Brooks glanced around to see if anyone had overheard. He'd told Graham a couple of months ago about Faith, in case the goalie had heard any rumors about a pregnant ex. But he'd sworn the man to secrecy, a secret Graham would take to his grave, after hurting Brooks as he had.

"We aren't playing half as good as these kids are," Graham remarked. "We can't without you. I've got no defense. No help at all out there."

Brooks gave a weary sigh. He wanted to celebrate with his new team. He appreciated his old teammates coming to the tournament in support, but he needed to let the kids know how great they'd played. So he was blunt with Graham. "I told you. I'm out this season." Then he turned back toward the locker room, but the goalie caught his shoulder.

"I didn't come here just to watch these kids show us up," Graham said. "I found out something you're gonna want to hear, Brooks."

His breath shuddered out with relief. He'd been waiting so long for this. "You figured out who Faith's mom is."

"Faith?" The confusion only increased.

"Faith is my daughter," Brooks reminded him.

"Seriously, man, are you sure she's yours? If you'd gotten some chick pregnant, she would have been all over you for child support."

He hadn't seen the results himself, but his dad had assured him that they'd come back and proved Faith was a Hoover. Brooks hadn't had to read a lab report to know she was his daughter. He'd felt it the first time he'd picked her up in his arms. "Yes, she's mine."

"Then you'd better get back to the league, so you can make some money to support her," Graham said.

Brooks had actually paid attention to his dad's lectures and hadn't blown the money he'd made over the years. He'd saved quite a bit, until a recent purchase. "Maybe next season…"

Graham shook his head. "Coach Stein's been calling you. He had a neurologist look at your scans. He thinks you could finish up this season."

"Stein never talked to me." Brooks had taken his coach's silence to mean that he didn't want him back on the team.

"He talked to your dad—several times." Graham snorted. "I figured you never got the message."

And apparently neither had his father when Brooks had told him he and his brothers needed to be responsible for their own lives. "Damn…"

"I need you back on the ice, protecting my ass. And there's no reason you can't come back."

Through the locker room door behind him, voices rose in celebration. And Priscilla would still be in the bleachers. He'd known exactly where she'd been sitting the entire game. Instead of her usual gray, she'd worn a red down jacket and a beautiful smile of pride and happiness. Was his dad really the only reason he hadn't been playing?

PRISCILLA DRAGGED A BREATH deep into her lungs and then lifted her fist to knock at the hotel room door. After a few seconds, Brooks opened it. His curls were disheveled, as if he'd been running his hands through them, and dark circles rimmed his brown eyes.

She pushed past him and walked inside, glad now that the school had rewarded the coach with a private room. She would have had one, too, if not for Maureen assuming they'd share.

Knocking hadn't been the hard part—making this admission was. But she forced the words from her lips. "I was wrong…maybe I was wrong about you. Maybe you are the man for me…if you want to be."

Brooks shut the door behind her and wearily leaned back against it. "I want *you*."

She released her breath in a shaky sigh and let her body sink into him. Her thighs pressed tight to his, and her breasts crushed against his chest. "I want you," she said.

His hands closed around her shoulders, but instead of pulling her closer, he eased her away from him. "I want you," he repeated, "but you deserve more, Priscilla."

Her heart constricted. When was she going to learn that she couldn't make someone love her?

"I'm sorry," she said, her face heating with embarrassment. "I thought you were starting to have feelings for me, too."

"I do have feelings for you," he said. "That's why I think you deserve more than I am. You were already married to one jerk. You shouldn't get involved with another one."

And ever since she'd been that gawky girl in high school, she had struggled with low self-esteem. She never would have thought a man like Brooks would suffer from it, too.

She cupped his face in her palms and looked straight into his eyes. "You are a good man, Brooks Hoover."

"No one's ever said that to me before." He moved away from the door and away from her. Then he reached for his wallet and pulled out a folded paper. "This is more like what I've usually been called."

Her fingers trembling, she took the note from his hand. Whatever was written on the paper had upset him. She read it to herself.

"Daddy. It's time for you to grow up and take some responsibility for once. You need to stop being a self-absorbed, selfish jerk and raise your daughter."

"Who wrote this?" she asked, studying the handwriting as much as the words. The curve of the letters seemed somehow familiar.

"Obviously, Faith's mother."

"It looks like a teenager wrote it."

Brooks snorted. "You think I'd have sex with a teenager? That's why I didn't show it to you earlier. I figured it would only make you think worse of me— but a teenager?"

"I'm sorry," Priscilla said. "It's just that I see kids' writing all the time. Besides, all this happened before you came home to Trout Creek."

"Trout Creek isn't my home," he said.

"It's where you grew up," she reminded him with a smile.

"I only came back because I had no place else to go," he told her.

"You have friends," she reminded him. "I saw them all—your former teammates—at the game tonight. You have other places you could have gone."

"You know the first thing I saw when I woke up from that coma?"

She shook her head. He hadn't talked much about that time with her.

"My dad. And this look on his face—" Brooks's voice cracked. "This love…"

"Your father does love you," she said, bracing herself to admit her own feelings for him. She didn't even care right now if he returned them; she just wanted to profess her love.

"Then why the hell does he mess with my life like he does?" Anger flushed Brooks's face. "I found out tonight that I could have been playing…. But my dad never let me know people were trying to get hold of me."

"I thought you were suspended for the season."

"Coach Stein got a second opinion from a neurologist who thinks I can play. He isn't worried about another concussion causing permanent damage."

"What?" Her stomach knotted with fear and dread. "You told me you were fine."

"I am now. I guess I always was."

"But that's not what you thought."

He shrugged. "I was told that I've had too many concussions. That if I took a hit like the last one, it might finish me."

An image of him lying lifelessly on the ice flashed through her mind. "No wonder your dad was worried."

Brooks pushed a hand through his hair again. "He worries about everything, mostly about losing me like he lost my mom."

Priscilla could identify with that. "But what if those first doctors were right, that playing again is too great a risk? Would you still play?"

Did he love the game so much that he would risk his life for it?

"I was going to get my own second opinion after I sat out this season. I intended to go back."

"Even if the risk was there?"

"It's all I know how to do," he admitted.

"No," she said. "Look what you've done for those kids."

"But it's all I've ever wanted to do," he reminded her.

She'd known that he would leave again, and she'd fallen for him anyway. "So you're going back? You're going to leave Trout Creek?" Leave her and Faith behind?

"I never intended to stay." And she had always known that.

"Right." She started backing toward the door.

"Priscilla, I'm sorry—"

"No, it's okay," she assured him. "You told me right from the beginning that this was just about having fun." Tears stung her eyes, but she blinked them away as she opened the door. Her voice cracking with emotion, she said, "I had fun."

"Priscilla—" His fingers brushed her shoulder as he reached for her, but she jerked away and ran into the hall, running past his brothers as the tears began to slide down her cheeks.

She had been such a fool to think that Brooks Hoover, of all men, would ever come to love her.

Chapter Sixteen

Despite his sunglasses cutting the glare of the sun off snow, Brooks had to squint as he peered out the windows of the bus. His head pounded more painfully than it had since he'd first awakened from the damn coma. He needed to talk to Priscilla, but she'd settled next to Debbie in the seat right behind the driver. And he'd been relegated to the back of the bus with the rowdiest kids.

Brad leaned over the seat in front of him. "Hey, Coach, what'd you do to Miss Andrews last night?"

Ryan joined his brother. "Yeah, what'd you do to make her cry? Did you tell her you don't have any feelings for her?"

Telling her that would have been a lie. "What do you know about it?" Brooks asked.

"We know you two have been going out for a while," Brad said. "Everybody knows."

"Is it serious?" Ryan asked.

His head pounded harder with regret and guilt. Brooks winced. "No."

At least it wasn't supposed to have been. He'd been so blinded with anger over his father's manipulations that he hadn't understood what she'd been trying to tell him last night. She'd thought he was a good man, the man for her. How could such a smart woman have been so wrong?

He wanted to be that man—the one she deserved. But if he went back to the game, he'd become the self-absorbed, selfish man Faith's mother had called him. And Priscilla deserved more.

"Then why was she crying?" Brad asked. "Tons of kids and parents, even teachers, have argued with her, but she never backs down."

Ryan nodded with respect. "Yeah, she's really tough."

"So was it because you're leaving?" Brad pressed.

"What?" Brooks turned back to his youngest brother. Had Graham said something to him?

"Was that what made her cry—that you're going to leave Trout Creek?" Brad asked again.

"What makes you so certain I'm going to leave?" Brooks wasn't so sure himself. Graham's news hadn't filled him with the relief and joy he'd expected. Instead it had torn him in two, dividing him between his old life and the new one he'd built for himself in Trout Creek. He'd started making plans for a future he'd never thought he could have.

Brad shrugged. "We watched the Eagles play last night. All the sportscasters were asking the team and the coaches about you. Your old coach said they were working on getting you back on board before the end of the season."

"Miss Andrews must have seen that, too," Ryan added. "So are you leaving before we finish up our season?"

Brooks gave a halfhearted smile. "I thought you wanted me to go back to playing. You think I'm too tough of a coach."

Brad jabbed his elbow into Ryan's side. "You don't want him to coach us? We never would have won the tournament with Cook at the helm."

"Hey," Brooks snapped, "how do you think I got to the tournament when I was at Trout Creek High? With Coach Cook guiding me."

"Yeah, like, a hundred years ago," Brad said.

Brooks laughed, then tensed as a female voice remarked, "That makes me feel old."

He glanced up at Maureen. "You have a tendency to age in the back of the bus," he warned her over the din of conversation, singing and arguments.

She dropped onto the seat next to him. "You do look like hell."

"Don't say I didn't warn you," he reminded her. "What brings you back here, anyway?" She had been sitting in the seat across from her sister and Debbie.

She grabbed his hand and dropped a few aspirin into his palm. "Knowing about your concussion and the noise level back here, Priscilla thought you might need these."

He turned toward the front and met Priscilla's gaze in the driver's wide mirror. Even though he'd been a jerk, she still cared about him. He was right; he didn't deserve her.

Having drained his water bottle already, he swallowed the tablets dry. "Tell her thanks."

"You could tell her yourself."

"If she wanted to talk to me, she wouldn't have sent you back with the aspirin," he pointed out.

Maureen chuckled. "Oh, maybe I'm not so old after all. Suddenly I feel like I'm back in junior high. 'You bring him this.' 'You tell her that.' You two need to talk to each other."

"Yes." But first he needed to talk to someone else.

BROOKS THREW OPEN the door to the sheriff's office, then slammed it behind him. "You had *no* right!"

The old man's shoulders sagged, almost as if a weight had been lifted from them. "You know."

"That you've been messing with my life again?" Brooks nodded. "I know now."

"Messing? I didn't think you felt like it was messed up anymore. I thought you were happy."

Brooks had been happy. A hell of a lot happier than he'd ever imagined he could be off the ice. Getting suspended wasn't the worst thing that had happened to him. Neither was coming back to Trout Creek.

"It's not that I don't like coaching..." He loved it. Watching those kids win had given him as much joy as playing himself ever had. "But I loved playing."

"Hockey?" Rex frowned. "I thought you were talking about Faith."

"Faith hasn't messed up my life," he said. His sleep, maybe, but it wasn't like he'd ever slept that much before. And he'd gotten more joy from her gassy smiles than from drinking too much and hooking up with random women. "You're the one who's messed up my life."

"Brooks, you were the one who caused that fight that nearly got you killed," his dad reminded him. "And when you interviewed for the coaching job, you didn't convince Priscilla to hire you. I just stepped in to fix the things you'd messed up for yourself."

Brooks sucked in a breath, offended and hurt that the old man thought so little of him. "Let me fix it myself."

"It's not broken anymore, son," his dad said with a grin. "It's perfect—or it will be once you settle down and get married. Priscilla is—"

"None of your business." Anger was gripping Brooks again. He wanted to throw things. Hell, if he'd been on the ice he would have thrown his stick and his helmet and then a punch. But he'd taught the kids better than that; he'd taught them control. Penalties only brought on power plays for the other team. He dragged in a deep, calming breath. "My life is my life. You have to stop trying to live it for me."

"It's just that I know what's better for you. I know what you need."

Brooks snorted, saddened as much as frustrated. "*I* know what I need."

"You didn't." The sheriff shook his head. "Until now. Until I got it for you."

Brooks couldn't deny his father's claim. Until he'd stepped off the bus at Trout Creek High tonight, he hadn't been certain of what he wanted. The opportunity to go back to his former life, the one he'd thought meant everything to him, had messed with his head, distracted him from what meant *everything* to him now.

"You got me the coaching job," he admitted. "But I

was the one who worked at it. I worked with those kids until they became winners. That was me." Maybe Ryan was right; maybe Coach Cook couldn't have done it. Trout Creek hadn't won a district tournament in years. And next week they had the state tournament.

But Coach Cook was probably recovered enough to take over now. His handshake had been firm and strong when he'd congratulated Brooks after the game.

"And you weren't even sure you wanted that job," the sheriff reminded him with an amused grin.

"But I stepped up," Brooks insisted. "Just like I did with Faith. No matter how much you and Myrtle helped, it was ultimately me taking care of Faith."

Rex bobbed his bald head in agreement, and there was a pride in his expression that Brooks couldn't remember seeing before. "You did."

"I could have walked away, just like Mom did—and believe me, I was tempted. But I'm not like her. Have I proved it to you yet?"

"You didn't have to prove to me what I already knew," his father retorted.

Just how many lies would the old man tell him to get what he wanted? "Yeah, right…"

"I may not have acted like it," his dad explained, "but I think I've always known. You had to prove it to yourself, though, that you're not like your mother."

Brooks shook his head as that tight knot of dread he'd lived with for so long eased. "I'm not. I'm not like her."

"That's right," his dad assured him, rising from his desk and coming around to grab Brooks's shoulders. "You're a damn good man."

Brooks closed his eyes as emotion overwhelmed him. Those words coming from his dad meant a lot, but the voice reverberating inside his head was Priscilla's. She'd said the same thing. And he hadn't listened. He hadn't believed her.

"You've stayed," his dad said, "for your team. And for a baby who isn't even yours."

Brooks's heart flipped, and he opened his eyes, stunned by his father's admission. "What?"

His father, always so fierce, stammered, "I—I thought you knew. I—I thought that was why you're so mad."

"Faith's not mine?" he asked. No, it wasn't true. It couldn't be true....

Rex shook his head.

"But that doesn't make sense. You said the DNA results proved that she's a Hoover."

His dad's throat convulsed, as if he were choking on all the damn lies he'd told. Then he clarified, "She's not *your* daughter."

"Then whose is she?"

"Mine," said a male voice, cracking with emotion. Ryan stepped inside the door. Priscilla stood behind him, hovering in the hall as if reluctant to intrude on this tense family moment.

But as the betrayal burned like acid in his stomach, Brooks lashed out—at her. Pushing past his brother, he caught her wrist in his hand. "*You* knew?"

Sympathy warmed her green eyes, which sparkled with tears. For him.

"Everyone knew but me," he realized. The child he had come to love as his own was his brother's daughter.

"I just figured it out," she said, "after you showed me the note. The handwriting looked familiar."

"Like a teenager's," he said, recalling her remark.

"Because it was a teenager's. It was Debbie's handwriting."

"Debbie?" The pain in his head pounded harder as he tried to process everything. He was reeling.

Her voice a gentle whisper, as if she knew how much he was hurting, Priscilla explained, "Debbie is Faith's mother."

And his brother was her father. Brooks was only her uncle. Even though he loved her as if she were his, she wasn't. Just as Priscilla wasn't, either, no matter the fantasies he'd begun to have about them—about them all being a family. That was what he'd figured out he'd wanted when the bus stopped in Trout Creek.

He'd wanted Priscilla as his wife, as the mother of his child. Now that nothing was as he'd believed it to be, his world shifted. He might as well have struck his head on the ice again, his brain was that addled. "I—I have to get out of here...."

He'd feared this ever since he'd come back to Trout Creek—feared that this sensation of walls falling in on him would come over him again, the way it had back in high school. That he'd feel as if a casket lid was closing, dirt being piled on his grave. "I—I can't stay...."

Hell, he couldn't breathe—couldn't process that once again his world had been turned upside down. Except that it had actually been turned right side up again. He could walk away. He had even fewer responsibilities than he'd had when he left his dad alone with two toddlers.

"SO YOU'RE LEAVING now?" Priscilla shouldn't have been surprised. He had no baby, no suspension, no reason to stay away from the ice. She certainly was no reason for him to remain here in Trout Creek.

"I have to…I need to get out of here." He pushed his hand through his hair, and his fingers trembled slightly. He glanced from her to his dad, then to his brother, as if he could hardly stand to look at any of them.

As if they had all betrayed him.

While her heart ached for him, she couldn't stop him. He had already been trapped in Trout Creek longer than he should have been. So she just held her breath until, with a groan of pain, Brooks turned and walked away.

She wasn't the only one who'd been holding her breath. Ryan gasped. And the sheriff dropped into the chair behind his desk and uttered a weary sigh. "I'm sorry about that, Miss Andrews. Brooks will come around. He'll understand."

"He might," she said, although she doubted it, "but I don't. So you all knew?"

Ryan lowered his head in shame and stared down at the floor. "Debbie told Brad on homecoming night, when he went over to talk to her. Then she told me. And we all told Dad."

"So you've all known for months that you're Faith's father," she stated, understanding now why Brooks had looked so utterly betrayed. "How could you have kept something so important from your brother?"

"We didn't know how to tell him," Ryan said. "So we told Dad first. But he already knew."

The sheriff lifted a ragged envelope from his desk. "The DNA results came back a while ago. They proved that Faith is a Hoover, but that Brooks is her uncle, not her father. Brad's too smart to get that serious with a girl at his age."

Ryan flinched as if his dad had slapped him. "But you didn't say anything to me until we came to you."

"You're not ready to be a father," the sheriff said.

Ryan pushed a hand through his curly hair, the same way his big brother always did. "And you thought Brooks was?"

"Not at first," the sheriff admitted, "but then he believed she was his, and the DNA test results hadn't come in yet. By the time they did, he'd stepped up— he'd proved himself."

"He'd fallen in love with her," Priscilla said.

And now he had lost her. Not like Priscilla had lost her baby, but she suspected it felt the same way. Permanent. And now Priscilla had lost him—before she'd ever really had him.

Chapter Seventeen

"So you're just gonna take off, then," Brad said, leaning against the jamb as Brooks tossed some stuff into his worn duffel bag.

"I have no reason to stay here." He should have been relieved; he should have felt lighter than he had in months.

"None?" Brad asked.

"You must have talked to Ryan." Brooks had been gone long enough, driving down all the back roads of Trout Creek. He suspected the whole town had heard he'd finally figured out he was living a lie. "You know the truth. I was the only one left in the dark."

"I'm sorry, Brooks, but you were doing the daddy thing really well," his brother said. "And Ryan—there's no way he could handle it. He's a screwup."

"He didn't mean for any of this to happen." Brooks couldn't help defending the sixteen-year-old.

"None of us meant for it to happen. But we didn't know how to tell you the truth without you getting mad. It was like it just snowballed, you know? And we didn't know how to stop it."

Their snowball of lies had knocked him down as hard as he'd been knocked down on the ice all those months ago. And he felt as confused.

"Do you really want to leave?" Brad asked.

No. But the pressure still weighed heavily on him, giving him that sense of panic and urgency. "I'm so sick of the old man manipulating me. I just need to get away from him."

"Is that what you want?" Brad asked. "Or are you just rebelling—doing the opposite of whatever Dad wants?"

Brooks's hand clenched the clothes he'd just shoved in the bag. "Is that what I've been doing?"

All those times he'd yelled at his father to stop treating him like a kid... Yet he still acted like one.

Brad shrugged. "I don't know what you're doing." He stared at Brooks for a moment. "Do you?"

Throwing away everything that mattered to him— that was what he'd be doing if he left. He needed to talk to his other brother. "Where's Ryan?"

"Dad took him over to the Cooks'. They're all going to talk about what's best for the baby."

"Without me?"

"Everybody thinks you've already taken off," Brad said.

"Of course." No matter what the old man had said, he still thought Brooks was just like his mother.

"I told Dad that you hadn't come back for your stuff," Brad continued, "but he said you're so mad you'd probably leave without it."

"I am mad." But he was more disappointed than

angry. Now. At first he'd been furious that his dad had played games and manipulated his life again. "I'm mad they don't think I have any say in what happens to Faith."

"But—but you really don't," Brad stammered as Brooks shoved past him in the doorway. "She's not yours."

Maybe not biologically. But she was his in every way that mattered, and his arms ached to hold her again. "Faith is my daughter."

Moments later, as he let himself into the Cooks' house, he repeated those exact words to the group assembled—and arguing—in the living room. And when the infant, clasped in Debbie's mother's arms, began to cry, he took the baby from her and held Faith close to his heart.

"Shh, sweetheart." With a heartfelt sigh, she settled against him and stared up at his face. "Daddy's here."

His father, perhaps knowing how badly he'd screwed up, stayed silent now. Even though he stood next to Ryan, he studied Brooks, as if unable to believe his oldest son was really there and not on the road leading away from Trout Creek.

"I don't care about the DNA," Brooks said. "I want to raise Faith." The baby might have been a surprise, but he could not imagine his life without her in it now. And she wasn't the only one he couldn't imagine a life without.

Debbie, her face red, her eyes puffy, glanced at Ryan, who looked as if he'd been crying, too. "Coach Hoover, she's yours. She should stay with you."

Brooks felt an overwhelming relief. "Are you sure?"

"You've been raising her. You've been taking care of her." Debbie's voice was shaky and she blinked back tears. "Good care of her."

Brooks looked down at the baby, content in his arms. During all those late nights of walking the floor and rocking, they had bonded like father and child. It didn't matter what the DNA results said. "That wasn't what I meant," he said to Debbie. "Are you sure you can give her up?"

The teenager nodded, and tears streaked down her face. "I already gave her up. I—I just left her there…on your doorstep. I don't deserve her."

Her mother stepped forward and slid an arm around her daughter's shoulders. "Debbie, I can't believe you went through all this alone. You should have told me. I would have helped you. We could have figured this out together."

Her face contorted with misery, Debbie shook her head. "I—I couldn't add to everything else you had going on." She glanced over to her grandfather, who stood near the windows. He was staring out at the lawn, his image reflected back at them, tears streaming from his eyes like his granddaughter's. "I couldn't tell you, Mom."

"You should have told me, D.," Ryan said, his voice shaking with emotion. "I should have known why you stopped talking to me, why you stopped hanging out." It was obvious now that Debbie's love hadn't been unrequited. "You quit the team. And I didn't know…"

"I couldn't tell you in person," Debbie admitted, "but I told you in that note I left with her."

A note Brooks had interpreted as being for him. But he didn't interrupt the kids to explain the misunderstanding. They were hurting so much. Given his own pain and self-pity earlier, he felt as self-centered and self-absorbed as the note had said.

"You should have told me when you first got pregnant," Ryan repeated. "You must have been so scared." The teenage defenseman who'd faced down opponents twice his size on the ice looked frightened to death now, his eyes wide, his face pale.

"What would you have done?" Debbie asked with a derisive snort. "Married me?"

Ryan swayed on his feet, and Brooks stepped closer, to steady him. But their father was there first, his hand on the boy's broad shoulder. "We're too young to get married," Ryan said.

"We're too young to be *parents*." Debbie turned back to Brooks and her baby. "Do you really want her?"

He nodded. "With my whole heart. I love her."

"You were thinking about giving her up," Ryan reminded him with a trace of bitterness, "when you thought she was yours."

"Because I love her, I want what's best for her," Brooks explained. "I wasn't sure then that that was me. Now I am sure."

Satisfied, Ryan nodded.

"I'm also sure that I want her to know you two are her biological parents."

"Won't it be weird?" Debbie asked.

"We'll figure it out," he promised. "She should know how special the two of you are. And how special she is." With a pointed stare at his father, he added, "I don't want any more lies or secrets in this family."

Faith Hoover would always know exactly who she was. It wouldn't take her thirty years to figure it out. He only hoped it wasn't too late for him.

Chapter Eighteen

"Are you okay?" Maureen asked, her elbows propped on the railing of Priscilla's front porch.

The March sun had chased away some but not all of the cold. Priscilla hardly noticed, though. She was numb. "I'm fine," she lied.

"Then why are you standing out here?" Maureen asked with a shiver. "You must be freezing."

"No. I need the fresh air to think," she said. And maybe she needed the cold to numb away the pain she'd felt earlier, in the sheriff's office.

"You're thinking about Brooks?"

She didn't bother denying it. "I'm trying to figure out who can take over as hockey coach. I don't think Coach Cook is recovered enough to bring them to the state championships."

"He looked pretty healthy at the game."

Priscilla shook her head, unable to envision Coach Cook in the job that had been his for so many years. Since Brooks had held that position, he had made it his own. Just as he'd made her his own. "You know, this is exactly why I didn't want him for the job. I knew he wouldn't stick it out. I just knew it...."

Tears choked her. She'd known he wasn't the man for her, either, but that hadn't stopped her from falling for him.

"That's not fair," a deep voice murmured. "You're just assuming that I'm taking off."

"You're not?" Maureen asked the question that was stuck in Priscilla's throat.

He lifted his arms, then dropped them back to his sides. "I'm here."

"For how long?" Maureen's voice was stern as she stepped into her role of overprotective older sister.

"That's up to Priscilla," he said. "Can I talk to her alone?"

Maureen waited until Priscilla nodded before leaving the porch for the path that led to the main lodge. He must have parked his vehicle there, since Priscilla hadn't heard him drive up.

"So you're going to turn in an actual resignation?" She shouldn't have been surprised. After all, he'd submitted an application with proper references—for a job he'd been all but guaranteed.

He shook his head. "Nope. If you want to get rid of me, you'll have to fire me. I'm not resigning."

"But—but..." she stammered in confusion. "How are you going to coach when you're leaving?"

"I'm not going anywhere," he assured her, his dark eyes alight with his usual mischief.

Was he just teasing her?

"But your coach got a neurologist to clear you to play again. You can go back."

"I talked to the coach. His neurologist still had concerns. I'd have to sign a waiver to play again—swear that I'm aware of the risk if I get another concussion."

"So there's still a risk?"

He nodded.

"Is it a risk you're willing to take to play the game you love?" she asked.

"No," he said.

"And you're fine with that? You've been dying to get back on the ice." She had been selfish to hope that he would give up what he loved for her and Faith.

"I'll get back out there," he said, "and start training again."

"With your team? So you're still leaving?" She was confused. He'd just said he wouldn't take the risk.

He shook his head. "*My* team is Trout Creek High. I need to be here for them."

"You're going to see the season through?" He really wasn't the man she'd initially judged him to be.

"Yeah."

"Things are going to change now," she pointed out. "Debbie and Ryan will have more responsibility. They might even have to give up hockey."

"They don't have to give up anything," he said. "They just need to be kids, and focus on growing up."

"Is Debbie's mom going to take Faith? Sonya is so busy with her dad." She stopped herself as realization dawned. "Your dad—of course. Your dad is going to take Faith."

Brooks shook his head. "No, the old man is not taking her. Faith is my daughter. Debbie and Ryan are going to make it official in an open adoption."

Priscilla shivered as the numbness began to fade, and she dared to hope.

"Here, let's go inside," he said, opening the door and guiding her with a hand on the small of her back. "It's cold out here."

She had argued that point with her sister, but the sun had begun to set, so she nodded.

Before closing the door, he grabbed a couple of split logs her brother-in-law had left on her porch. Then he started a fire in the small stone hearth in the corner of her living room.

As the room began to warm, she shrugged off her jacket and stepped closer to the blaze and Brooks. "You're really going to adopt Faith?"

He unzipped his jacket and dropped it onto the back of the plaid couch. Then he joined her in front of the fire, his grin brighter than the flames. "Yes."

"Brooks, are you sure?"

"Everyone keeps asking me that," he said with a chuckle.

"With good reason," she pointed out. "It's a big decision. You're taking on responsibility for another life— for the rest of your life. Have you really thought this through?"

"Yes," he replied, his voice absolutely certain.

"But it's only been a few hours since you found out she's not yours."

"She's mine. She's been mine since the first time I picked her up." His words were gruff with emotion. "There's only one thing in this life—in my life—that I've been more sure about than adopting Faith."

"What's that?" Priscilla asked, although she thought she knew. Hockey. Back in high school, she had never seen anyone as certain of what he would be doing with his life.

"That I love you," he said. When her mouth dropped open, he pressed his thumb against her chin to push it shut and then pulled her into his arms. "And I want to spend the rest of my life with you."

"Brooks!" she exclaimed, unable to believe what he was saying. She'd known he was the man for her, but hadn't dared to dream he could love her the way she longed to be loved.

"And yes, I'm sure." He laughed and tightened his arms around her. "I want to marry you, Priscilla Andrews."

She shook her head, unable to process what he was saying. Was she imagining it all? Had she cried herself to sleep over his leaving and dreamed this whole encounter? She reached up to check if he was real, rubbing her fingertips along the short stubble on his jaw.

He caught her hand and pressed her knuckles against his lips. "I don't have a ring yet, or I'd drop down on my knees and offer it to you. You deserve all that—the big romantic proposal. And I'll give that to you when I get the ring. But I wanted to apologize for being such a jerk earlier, at my dad's office."

"You'd just been dealt a couple major blows," she said. "You were reeling. You felt betrayed."

"You didn't betray me. And I never should have yelled at you. I'm so sorry."

She smiled. "You could have just sent me flowers. You don't have to propose."

"That's not why I proposed," he said, his gaze intent on her face. "I'm serious, Priscilla. I want to spend my life with you. But what do you want?"

She hadn't dared to hope for more than he'd already given her. More fun and pleasure than she'd ever known. But because she loved him, she couldn't let him give up the one thing that had always been so much a part of him. "I can't ask you to give up your career. You love hockey."

"Yes," he admitted. "And that's why I love coaching it."

"But you love playing."

"Are you trying to get rid of me?" he asked. "I know that you didn't think—when we first started this—that I was the guy for you. But when you came to me at the hotel, I thought you'd started to see *me*. I've become a different man since coming home. Do you want that man, Priscilla?"

With her whole heart. "But one day you might regret—"

"I won't," he assured her. "And you have yet to answer me."

"I will marry you," she agreed.

He scooped her up in his arms and swung her around. "Oh, thank God—thank *you!*"

"As if anyone could ever tell Brooks Hoover no," she teased.

"You did," he reminded her. "When you wouldn't hire me."

"I think I want to offer you another job," she said.

"Husband? I can't give you any references, but I promise to work really hard."

She smiled. "You're already hired for that. I want you to be the athletic director."

"Are you sure?"

She nodded. "Then I can spend more time taking care of your daughter."

"*Our* daughter," he interjected. "I want you to adopt her with me."

She tensed with dread as a horrible suspicion occurred to her. "You haven't—that isn't why you're asking me, is it? Because you promised the Cooks that you'd find a mother for Faith?"

Stung by her mistrust, Brooks loosened his grip on her. She slid down, soft and warm against his tense body. But he stepped back and shoved his hands into his jeans pockets so he wouldn't reach for her again and show her how much he needed her. She had to be certain on her own. "You think I'm using you?"

"Are you?" she asked, with a fearful gasp that betrayed her insecurity.

Knowing she'd been hurt, he pushed aside his own pain at her doubts. "No. I convinced the Cooks to let me adopt Faith because I love her."

In the end, that was all the convincing Debbie's mother had needed—that and an assurance that she would be part of the baby's life, too. If Priscilla had flat-out turned down his proposal, he wouldn't be raising his baby girl alone. He had more than an extended family to help him; he had the whole damn town of Trout Creek.

"I never mentioned you," he continued. "I had no idea if you would accept my proposal or not. If you still feel this way about me, that I can't be trusted—that I'm a user—why did you accept?"

She lifted her slender shoulders in a brief shrug, and her eyes glistened with tears. "I love you, Brooks."

He bit his bottom lip so that he wouldn't automatically say the words back. And he fisted his hands in his pockets so that he wouldn't grab her. Instead he reminded them both, "But you don't trust me."

"It's not you I don't trust."

"Are you sure you don't think I'm still that idiot I was back in high school? Or the playboy hothead before I took that last fall on the ice?"

"No, I know you're a good man."

"Then why don't you trust that I want you?" he asked, his frustration building.

"I don't trust *happiness,*" she explained. "I thought I had it before, only to have it all fall apart. I just need to be sure that you're marrying me for me, not because there's a baby involved."

"I love *you,* Priscilla," he said, finally pulling his hands from his pockets. He stepped closer to her. "Sure, I know that you'll be the best mother that little girl could have, but I'm not marrying you for her. I'm marrying you for me—because you make me happy."

She gasped again, that little betrayal of her doubt. "I do?"

His hands trembling, he cupped her face. His voice shook with everything he felt for her as he told her, "You are the most incredible woman I've ever met. You're sexy and smart and compassionate—and passionate. You're more than I deserve—"

"No, Brooks—"

He stemmed her protest with a finger on her silky lips. "But because I know that, you make me try harder, so that someday I might deserve you."

Her lips moved against his fingers as she breathed his name again.

"You make me better than I ever thought I could be," he added.

"I don't deserve you," she murmured. Then she rose up on her toes and pressed her mouth to his.

He tasted her tears and felt a rush of guilt that he'd made her cry. But when he opened his eyes to look at her, he had never seen anyone as happy as she was. She glowed with joy and love and trust.

"No," he agreed. "You deserve so much more. But I'll get that for you. I'll get you whatever you want." He should have waited to propose until he'd bought her a ring. "I'll get you a diamond," he promised. "And a house."

She shook her head. "I already have everything I want. You."

"And Faith?"

"Of course I want Faith," she assured him. "Every time I picked her up, I felt like she was mine. I felt like we all belonged together."

"Here in Trout Creek," he said.

"You're sure?" she asked again. "You hated living here when we were growing up. You felt suffocated."

That pressure was off his chest now. "I'm certain. So certain that I already bought the Icehouse."

"You're taking on an awful lot of responsibility, Mr. Hoover," she cautioned.

He breathed deeply and easily. "I can handle it. With you as my wife, I can handle anything."

* * * * *

Harlequin Intrigue top author
Delores Fossen presents
a brand-new series of breathtaking
romantic suspense!
TEXAS MATERNITY: HOSTAGES
The first installment available May 2010:
THE BABY'S GUARDIAN

Shaw cursed and hooked his arm around Sabrina.

Despite the urgency that the deadly gunfire created, he tried to be careful with her, and he took the brunt of the fall when he pulled her to the ground. His shoulder hit hard, but he held on tight to his gun so that it wouldn't be jarred from his hand.

Shaw didn't stop there. He crawled over Sabrina, sheltering her pregnant belly with his body, and he came up ready to return fire.

This was obviously a situation he'd wanted to avoid at all cost. He didn't want his baby in the middle of a fight with these armed fugitives, but when they fired that shot, they'd left him no choice. Now, the trick was to get Sabrina safely out of there.

"Get down," someone on the SWAT team yelled from the roof of the adjacent building.

Shaw did. He dropped lower, covering Sabrina as best he could.

There was another shot, but this one came from a rifleman on the SWAT team. Shaw didn't look up, but he heard the sound of glass being blown apart.

The shots continued, all coming from his men, which

meant it might be time to try to get Sabrina to better cover. Shaw glanced at the front of the building.

So that Sabrina's pregnant belly wouldn't be smashed against the ground, Shaw eased off her and moved her to a sitting position so that her back was against the brick wall. They were close. Too close. And face-to-face.

He found himself staring right into those sea-green eyes.

How will Shaw get Sabrina out?
Follow the daring rescue and the heartbreaking
aftermath in THE BABY'S GUARDIAN
by Delores Fossen,
available May 2010 from Harlequin Intrigue.

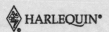

HARLEQUIN *Presents*

Bestselling Harlequin Presents® author

Lynne Graham

introduces

VIRGIN ON HER WEDDING NIGHT

Valente Lorenzatto never forgave Caroline Hales's
abandonment of him at the altar. But now he's
made millions and claimed his aristocratic Venetian
birthright—and he's poised to get his revenge.
He'll ruin Caroline's family by buying out their
company and throwing them out of their mansion...
unless she agrees to give him the wedding night
she denied him five years ago....

**Available May 2010
from Harlequin Presents!**

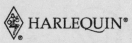

Former bad boy Sloan Hawkins is back in
Redemption, Oklahoma, to help keep his aunt's
cherished garden thriving and to reconnect with the
girl he left behind, Annie Markham. But when he
discovers his secret child—and that single mother
Annie never stopped loving him—he's determined
that a wedding will take place in the garden
nurtured by faith and love.

REDEMPTION
❧RIVER❧

Where healing flows...

Look for

The Wedding Garden
by Linda Goodnight

Available May 2010
wherever you buy books.

Steeple
Hill®

LI87595

REQUEST YOUR FREE BOOKS!
2 FREE NOVELS PLUS 2 FREE GIFTS!

HARLEQUIN®

American Romance®

Love, Home & Happiness!

YES! Please send me 2 FREE Harlequin® American Romance® novels and my 2 FREE gifts (gifts are worth about $10). After receiving them, if I don't wish to receive any more books, I can return the shipping statement marked "cancel." If I don't cancel, I will receive 4 brand-new novels every month and be billed just $4.24 per book in the U.S. or $4.99 per book in Canada. That's a saving of at least 15% off the cover price! It's quite a bargain! Shipping and handling is just 50¢ per book.* I understand that accepting the 2 free books and gifts places me under no obligation to buy anything. I can always return a shipment and cancel at any time. Even if I never buy another book from Harlequin, the two free books and gifts are mine to keep forever.

154/354 HDN E5LG

Name _____ (PLEASE PRINT)

Address _____ Apt. #

City _____ State/Prov. _____ Zip/Postal Code

Signature (if under 18, a parent or guardian must sign)

Mail to the **Harlequin Reader Service:**
IN U.S.A.: P.O. Box 1867, Buffalo, NY 14240-1867
IN CANADA: P.O. Box 609, Fort Erie, Ontario L2A 5X3

Not valid for current subscribers to Harlequin® American Romance® books.

Want to try two free books from another line?
Call 1-800-873-8635 or visit www.morefreebooks.com.

* Terms and prices subject to change without notice. Prices do not include applicable taxes. N.Y. residents add applicable sales tax. Canadian residents will be charged applicable provincial taxes and GST. Offer not valid in Quebec. This offer is limited to one order per household. All orders subject to approval. Credit or debit balances in a customer's account(s) may be offset by any other outstanding balance owed by or to the customer. Please allow 4 to 6 weeks for delivery. Offer available while quantities last.

Your Privacy: Harlequin is committed to protecting your privacy. Our Privacy Policy is available online at www.eHarlequin.com or upon request from the Reader Service. From time to time we make our lists of customers available to reputable third parties who may have a product or service of interest to you. ☐ If you would prefer we not share your name and address, please check here.

Help us get it right—We strive for accurate, respectful and relevant communications. To clarify or modify your communication preferences, visit us at www.ReaderService.com/consumerchoice.

HAR10R

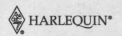
HARLEQUIN®

Showcase

On sale May 11, 2010

Reader favorites from the most talented voices in romance

Save $1.00 on the purchase of 1 or more Harlequin® Showcase books.

SAVE $1.00 on the purchase of 1 or more Harlequin® Showcase books.

Coupon expires Oct 31, 2010. Redeemable at participating retail outlets. Limit one coupon per purchase. Valid in the U.S.A. and Canada only.

52609015

Canadian Retailers: Harlequin Enterprises Limited will pay the face value of this coupon plus 10.25¢ if submitted by customer for this product only. Any other use constitutes fraud. Coupon is nonassignable. Void if taxed, prohibited or restricted by law. Consumer must pay any government taxes. Void if copied. Nielsen Clearing House ("NCH") customers submit coupons and proof of sales to Harlequin Enterprises Limited, P.O. Box 3000, Saint John, NB E2L 4L3, Canada. Non-NCH retailer—for reimbursement submit coupons and proof of sales directly to Harlequin Enterprises Limited, Retail Marketing Department, 225 Duncan Mill Rd., Don Mills, ON M3B 3K9, Canada.

U.S. Retailers: Harlequin Enterprises Limited will pay the face value of this coupon plus 8¢ if submitted by customer for this product only. Any other use constitutes fraud. Coupon is nonassignable. Void if taxed, prohibited or restricted by law. Consumer must pay any government taxes. Void if copied. For reimbursement submit coupons and proof of sales directly to Harlequin Enterprises Limited, P.O. Box 880478, El Paso, TX 88588-0478, U.S.A. Cash value 1/100 cents.

® and TM are trademarks owned and used by the trademark owner and/or its licensee.
©2009 Harlequin Enterprises Limited

HSCCOUP0410

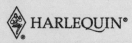

HARLEQUIN®

COMING NEXT MONTH

Available May 11, 2010

#1305 THE BABY TWINS
Babies & Bachelors USA
Laura Marie Altom

#1306 THE MAVERICK
Texas Outlaws
Jan Hudson

#1307 THE ACCIDENTAL SHERIFF
Fatherhood
Cathy McDavid

#1308 DREAM DADDY
Daly Thompson

www.eHarlequin.com